RENDEZVOUS AT THE ALTAR

RENDEZVOUS AT THE ALTAR

From Vietnam to Virginia

THUAN LE ELSTON

Rand-Smith Books www.rand-smith.com

Print ISBN: 978-1-950544-29-5
Digital ISBN: 978-1-950544-28-8
First Printing, 2021

Rand-Smith Books
Rand-Smith LLC
Ashland, VA
www.rand-smith.com

Contents

v

One

January 28, 2009

To all my children, my futures, my afterlives,

Where are you?

Are you alone? Are you home, or in transit?

Are you happy? Maybe more important, how do you feel about your pursuit of happiness? Have you earned it, courted it? Or have you had to pursue it in the fourteenth century definition, as in tracking down a fugitive?

It's a Wednesday, hours from dawning. You're all in bed, exhausted after a long weekend of traveling across the country for the funeral of my maternal grandmother in Phoenix. She was the last of your great-grandmothers to pass away, and I can't help comparing her life with the others: Four women, two from Vietnam and two from America. Yet what strikes me is that the two Vietnamese shared a culture but lived very differently, and that the two Americans might as well have come from different planets.

I've been thinking a lot of my grandparents, your great-grandparents. I've been thinking of their beginnings and endings. What I think I know anyway, from what I've learned of well-traveled family anec-

dotes, photographs, and genealogy records. I don't remember the first time I saw my grandparents, but I do remember meeting your daddy's. Each time, I was very conscious of the fact that I was laying eyes on a stranger whose DNA would help to intimately dictate who my children would be. Even after all these years, I marvel at each encounter: To enter a room accompanying the man I wanted to spend the rest of my life with and meet his past, as well as my future.

I'm finally ready to tell you the stories of your great-grandmothers, though I don't know when you'll be ready to read this. It doesn't matter. No matter how many years after I type these words, and no matter where you are right now, what matters is that you've decided it's time to meet your past.

Your only Mẹ Mẹ

Two

ANNE JAQUELINE ELEY
(born November 12, 1916)

She was lying on a white bed with her eyes closed. He couldn't describe it as sleeping because he didn't know. It wasn't as if he could ask her. He hoped she was sleeping. Or playing possum. Was she awake? Could she still dream?

The young man wondered whether he should speak up, just start talking to his grandmother about his hour-plus drive from his parents' place outside L.A. down to the edge of San Diego. His parents had wanted him to visit Nanny with them yesterday, but he couldn't make it because of his job as a freelancer for the *Los Angeles Times*. It had been crazy at work these past couple of months since a jury acquitted all those cops in the Rodney King case. Not that the editors would send a cub reporter so white like him into the riot zones of L.A., but even in the *Times* bureau in Orange County, just south of all the action, there had been plenty of work. And even if there weren't, where would he rather be at a time like this than in a newsroom anyway?

He opened his mouth to tell Nanny about it all but suddenly felt shy in front of her, or maybe just silly. Instead, he yawned and stood up to stretch his arms and legs. He liked driving, but man ...

He wandered around the room that — despite the light streaming through the window, the rosy curtains, the flowered wallpaper, the framed nautical prints — couldn't bring itself to be anything but a sterile hospice room. Outside the window below was a cemetery camouflaged in such a perfect green lawn that Nanny, when awake, mistook it for a golf course, a mistake that — without discussion — no one in the family had corrected, not even his younger brother with the dry sense of humor. Maybe especially his brother.

He turned from the window to look back at her. She was so silent, the only way he was sure she was breathing was from the Darth Vader-worthy noises coming from the machines hooked up to her.

"Nanny?" Just a test, to see how it felt to speak to someone in a coma. Could she hear him? You read about all those anecdotes, but how can you know until you're in a coma yourself? On top of it all, before allowing him into this room, a hospice nurse warned him that Nanny's eyes might open but she wouldn't respond, that this had been happening. How does that play into consciousness? What was he supposed to do? "Nanny, I brought you some cigarettes."

Nothing. Not a sound from that voice deepened by a lifetime of smoking. The last time he saw her, the white-haired woman's eyes had lit up at the sight of the forbidden smokes, her wrinkled mouth giggling as if she were a little kid about to sneak off with some marshmallows.

He wandered back to the chair beside her bed, drawing in his head a diagram of family ties. There was him, Bob, and next to him was his younger brother. Above them were their parents, his father's siblings, his mother's sister, all their children below them. Above his father were *his* parents, Hal and Mary, living in Colorado. And above his mother were *her* parents, Carroll, deceased, and Anne, whose time, by all indications, had come.

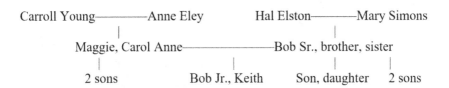

Bob pondered that diagram in his head, looking at it from all sides. Who were the people above Nanny? For that matter, he was unfamiliar with any of his grandparents' siblings or his great-grandparents and their origins. Where did they all come from? What about the ancestors before them?

He hadn't always wondered about the word "ancestor." Back in his freshman year in high school in Chippewa Falls, Wisconsin, a teacher had gone around the room asking for everyone's roots. One by one, his classmates had reeled off their heritage: Norwegian, Scottish, Irish, Polish, German. When she got to him, he shrugged and said, "I'm from America," and everyone laughed. Since then, he had left the Midwest far behind. While studying at American University in Washington, D.C., he interned for the Japanese Embassy, and one of his jobs was to report on the Senate hearings of the Tiananmen Square massacre in China that summer of '89. Those hearings inspired him to stop taking Japanese as his foreign language and pick up Chinese. When he moved to Southern California and attended USC, he found a program that allowed him to spend his summers studying Mandarin in China and teaching English in Taiwan.

For the Chinese, it was all about bloodlines. Getting to know his Chinese friends meant being introduced to an extended clan for which his family hadn't prepared him. Take his limited family-tree diagram, for example. It went back to his grandparents and that was it. It was nothing like tracing your roots back to X dynasty or Y village or ... whatever. He knew so little about the ancestral branches above him, and now Nanny's dying. Why the hell didn't he pick her brain about her lineage while she was still lucid?

He squeezed her hand and nearly jumped out of his skin when her eyes suddenly, but slowly, opened. "Nanny?"

Silence. Not even a grunt from that throaty voice. He took a deep breath to slow his heart and squeezed her hand again. *Say something. She might be able to hear you. She might be able to see you.*

"Can you see me, Nanny? It's Bob, one of your grandsons. Can you hear me? I ... I finally saw the smoke from the riots, Nanny."

Bob.

"It's just great to see your eyes, Nanny. I'll talk for the both of us, all right? OK, Nanny? Just keep looking at me. I ... I've been working, Nanny, since the riots happened but, you know, from the local angle down in Orange County. The *L.A. Times* has plenty of star reporters. They don't need me. I'm just a freelancer barely out of college. But they pulled all the African American reporters from our bureau and all the other bureaus, too, to go work South Central L.A. I guess they figured some areas are too dangerous to send in white reporters right now."

Quit ... quit squeezing ... What ...

"I drove up to Pasadena to see a friend, and you can see the smoke rising from the highways. Pockets of them. It's like driving over a war zone."

... in God's name. Am I in danger? I just nod off for a little bit, and the whole world goes to hell. They never tell me what goes on anymore. Anybody that does anything for me in this hospice is black, I mean African American. I think I've — I've been nice to them. My mother taught me that, to always be nice to our black house staff in Norfolk. You never know what they say behind you. That's harmless. Who of significance would believe them anyway? It's what they might do behind you.

"Nanny, can you see me?"

You. Tell me you're here to get me out! Is your mom out there doing the paperwork? Where will I go? They were all African Americans at the last place, too, and even in the hospital. Hispanics, I mean, wait, Latinos. Filipinos. I give up. Don't white people go into nursing anymore?

"I don't know what those jurors were thinking, Nanny. It's really tragic. It's like, I'm almost ashamed to be white."

Well, I'll be! I'll be a monkey's uncle! If Carroll could hear one of his grandsons saying such a thing. You can stop right there ... you can leave.

"I think I told you, Nanny, after Rodney King was beaten last year? You were still at the nursing home, remember? I told you about how I was volunteering at a high school in South Central?"

HA. You mean when I could still go to the bathroom by myself? Barely. When I was still considered to be among the living instead of this, this almost-dead. God. I remember you, chatting up the nurse and waiting until she left the room. Palmed me a pack of Winstons. Then you read to me. News stories. How many blows, batons, how many officers there were. I remember you reading that that big black man was on drugs. I remember calling you out on that.

At least your visits are tolerable, even those times when you wouldn't buy me Winstons until I agreed to go out for a ride with you. Your mom, when she was still bringing me cigarettes, knew not to bring me any other brand. Because of our R.J. Reynolds stocks. But somewhere, she stopped letting me have any fun. She was so cross that time I got out on my own and tried to look for a bus. I had to get back to Norfolk. I figured a bus ride from here to Virginia ...

Or was it Florida?

To go back. In place and in time. Chiffon dresses, dancing, playing tennis. It's getting so I even miss gauzy, clingy heat. I still have people there who'd take care of me. Two sisters. A brother. Or their children. I'm sure they had children. I know one of my sisters worked for AA. My father died of alcoholism. Wait, no! He, I remember now, he died of a heart attack after hearing that the Japanese had bombed Pearl Harbor.

Go back to the South! I haven't wanted to return there for a long time. Carroll found me, took me away. And I never looked back.

Somebody must have turned me in! I swear, Carroll, I can't trust anyone, not anymore. You can no longer bank on it, hospitality. They found me before I could find a bus going east. Dragged me to that, that HOME. Assisted living. SPIT on that! Nursing home. Spit! It's just an old-people place my daughters put me in.

And now here. Boy, what IS this here and now? I open my eyes, you're talk-

ing. Tall fuzzy redhead. I want to open your hands and see a pack of Winstons, or even Salems. I'm feeling shaky, can't you see? Menthol will also do, dear, 'cause I think I have a cold. At least a cold. A hot brandy would help, with some honey and a little lemon in it. But I can't have liquor, either. Not allowed anything anymore. Where's the fun in that?

"I'll admit, Nanny, I was nervous returning to that high school the day news broke that Rodney King was beaten by those white cops. The school's all black. Would those kids take out their anger on the first white face they saw? Would anyone show up for my journalism class? But get this, none of the students gave any hint they had seen the video running on a loop on the local news. Students showed up for my class as if nothing happened. By the end of class, I couldn't stand it anymore. I asked them about it. And you know what? They're like, black men get beaten all the time by cops. That isn't news to us! And these are fifteen, sixteen, seventeen-year-olds. I was so innocent at their age, Nanny, growing up in Wisconsin. I'm not much of an adult even now. They should be worrying about Friday night football and whatever else teenagers get excited about, not getting beaten on the side of the street for their skin color! How can we, the richest, most democratic nation on earth, have kids grow up this way?"

You're much more fun as an adult than you were a child, you know that? Let's face it. I didn't enjoy any of my grandchildren that much. I'm sorry, but y'all were so noisy, and always movin' and wantin'. I got exhausted just looking at you running 'round our house whenever you visited.

My girls ... they're all right. They weren't terrible children. As adults, I think we hurt their feelings 'cause we never visited your families that much. Well, I'm sorry, but yours was living in Wisconsin at the time for God's sake. Your aunt and your cousins were in Florida. Listen, your grandfather was retired, and we had all these places to see. He worked hard all his life, earned the right to do all the things he wanted to before he died. You can't hold that against us.

Anne Eley inhaled as if it hurt and turned ever so slightly away from the young man, her light eyes fluttering before the paper-thin lids closed over the pupils. "Nanny?" His fingers flew to her wrist.

Pulse still there. What a relief. But maybe he's tiring her. Is she sick of his rambling on and on? Had she gone back to sleep? Or did she not like the conversation they were having? He wasn't willing to give up yet, though. He was just getting comfortable talking to her, just starting to feel natural.

"You wouldn't believe it, Nanny, but they didn't hold it against me at all, any of this injustice that they take for granted. One girl even asked me to take her to the prom! I was so flattered, and I was going to do it. If she had the guts to ask a college guy, and look beyond skin color to ask me, then I wanted to take her. But her age stopped me. I would have felt like a pervert. Can you imagine her parents' reaction if I drove to her house to pick her up, Nanny? That would have been classic."

Still here? Just don't expect me to look at you. Eyes tired.

Sigh. Honey, I think you underestimated the girl, I really do. Maybe she knew you'd be the safest date she can have and still have that caché of taking an older man. Compare yourself with the boys at her school. Unassuming, you are. Just blending right in, making yourself at home anywhere and not bothering anyone. Non-threatening; those glasses. You should hear the nurses talk after your visits. They're always saying what a nice, friendly grandson I have, and telling me I'm lucky you come to see me. I guess it's your open face, big smile.

Funny how they never mention your T-shirts, obnoxious things from those — what do you call them? — PUNK concerts you and your brother go to. Rancid. What kind of a band name is that? Meat Puppets. Circle Jerks. What does that even mean? One band name I actually liked was Green Day, and the girl on the shirt you wore even had a green hairband. On the other hand, she was holding a smoking gun! Why?

"How are you doing, Mrs. Young? You don't want to know the day I've had. That sound you're hearing is just me pulling my chair closer, Mrs. Young. I hope you are enjoying what I have been reading to you. It's 'The Prime of Miss Jean Brodie' by Muriel Spark. Remember? It is an escape for me, too. And trust me, I need it. I think this is where I left off. You ready?

"'Rose,' said Miss Brodie, 'is like a heroine from a novel by D.H.

Lawrence. She has got instinct.' But in fact, the art master's interest in Rose was simply a professional one, she was a good model; Rose had an instinct to be satisfied with this role, and in any event, it was Sandy who slept with Teddy Lloyd and Rose who carried back the information."

What happened to my grandson? How long, how long have you been reading to me?

"'He interests me,' said Sandy.

"'Interests you, forsooth,' said Miss Brodie. 'A girl with a mind, a girl with insight. He is a Roman Catholic and I don't see how you can have to do with a man who can't think for himself. Rose was suitable. Rose has instinct but no insight.'"

You again. These hospice volunteers! Did I sign a waiver? Maybe one of my daughters. Can't open my eyes. Haaahhh hahummmmm. Excuse me. Was I yawning? Sorry, but aren't we almost done with this book? The Prime of Miss Jean Brodie *was a pretty good movie if I remember right, but Carroll couldn't stand that Jean. "Women shouldn't be where they shouldn't be," he used to say. I never paid much attention to the book until you and your reading.*

"Teddy Lloyd continued reproducing Jean Brodie in his paintings. 'You have instinct,' Sandy told him, 'but no insight, or you would see that the woman isn't to be taken seriously.'

"'I know she isn't,' he said. 'You are too analytical and irritable for your age.'

"The family had returned, and their meetings were dangerous and exciting. The more she discovered him to be still in love with Jean Brodie, the more she was curious about the mind that loved the woman. By the end of the year, it happened that she had quite lost interest in the man himself, but was deeply absorbed in his mind, from which she extracted, among other things, his religion as a pith from a husk. Her mind was as full of his religion as a night sky is full of things visible and invisible. She left the man and took his religion and became a nun in the course of time."

Now that's what I call going around Kelly's barn. This Sandy was supposed to be so educated, yet she had never heard of the shortest route being a straight line?

Child, speak up. Why the mumbling all of a sudden? You're not doing it on purpose, are ya? Playing a trick on an old woman? You don't seem the type. Child, why can't I hear you anymore? I don't even know your name. You said it the first time you came in here, I think. But what is it? I'm sorry, honey, especially after you introduced yourself with such good manners. I remember that. I don't expect good manners these days, not these days, and not outside the South. That's why I remembered you. But really, you can't blame me for not remembering your name. When was the last time you said your name again before you started reading? I just wake up and your voice is there and it takes up the whole room.

I could read YOU some literature for a change. I don't even need a book; it's all up here in my head. I used to entertain my girls by reciting long passages from Robert Service. You know his poetry? How about his The Shooting of Dan McGrew? *It's an epic. It has a life of its own.*

What are you studying in school? I suppose literature. Or not. My daughters keep telling me that you shouldn't assume anything in this day and age. They should talk, let me tell you.

Are you a nursing student? Learning your bedside manner? You don't sound colored. I mean ... really, that should cover black and brown, shouldn't it? Aren't Filipinos brown? Their names sound Spanish. God, I should know this. I've traveled. I'm not your typical Ugly American, I swear.

❋❋❋

Listen, my hospice volunteer, my dear reader, you think it was easy being a normal girl back then? No. We weren't allowed to study much. I chose nutrition or some such useful thing. All wives have to learn how to feed their families wholesome meals and balance a food budget, so my family thought it was proper enough. But I got to go all the way to Florida for school. It was all right; we had people there. I forget whether they were on my mother's side or my father's. But it was at the home of a friend of the family where I met Carroll.

Carroll Raymond Young was raised in Omaha and educated at the University of Illinois. He was living in New York. Or was it New Jersey? Anyway, he traveled to Florida a lot for his insurance job at Continental. Is it still around?

He was a full eight years older than me and already had a past. A wife, to be exact, who died from an illness. I was told by our mutual friends that her death devastated him. Carroll didn't want me asking questions. Oh, he eventually told me about her, but he didn't want me talking about her to our girls. Ever. I only told our eldest when she got married because she was moving to Florida and I was afraid that our old family friends who had introduced me to Carroll would mention it.

I mean, he was just very private about it and considered it nobody else's business but his own. When I met him, he was just known as a successful businessman and a sophisticated traveler. All the girls and their mothers had their eyes on him. Being tall, dark, and handsome didn't hurt, either. Compare him with the boys I was used to!

He would travel back and forth from New York to Florida, and there'd be long absences and lots of letters. I lived for those letters, his stories about things not of the South. I couldn't believe he'd want someone like me, a product of Norfolk, Virginia, and not some fashionable Northern girl. But he did. We married on our ninth date. And I was excited to get out. I wanted to see the world with this worldly man.

New York was not Norfolk. Even if its streets led to the water like Norfolk's did, it was a different body of water. New York did not revolve around the Navy; it was no small town.

Carroll soon moved me to an even more foreign place: Northern California. And there, the Pacific Ocean even smelled different to me. How many people from Norfolk got to see more than the old Atlantic that was practically outside our front door? Only the ones who joined the Navy, that's how many. The Navy was the biggest employer for miles around. And here's me: I didn't have to turn sailor and I was clear on the other side of the country.

I was living in a postcard. Carroll's job was a good one, and we lived well. The two girls came one after another, Maggie and Carol Anne, the youngest named after both Carroll and me. Soon, we could afford to move right outside San Francisco into a pretty, hilly suburb called Millbrae. I was playing house, and it was everything I thought I wanted. A sophisticated, modern life.

Those cocktail parties, though. God, the first one I went to, I was terrified. My accent, fresh from the South ... not knowing what they knew. Even if I *were* brave enough to talk, what would I talk to them about? I had nothing in common with them. Getting ready for that first party, I changed my dress so often Carroll finally came into the bedroom and gave me a drink.

And the drinks definitely helped. Lord, they were a lifesaver. At a party, you can't go wrong with a glass of something in one hand and a cigarette in the other. Some people even claimed that my accent was genteel. Imagine. The men loved it. More than a few told me they liked the way I made them feel as if we were socializing in the old days. Though I don't know what kind of old days they were talking about. Maybe plantation life or something, making up whatever they didn't know with what they read in books or saw in the picture show. Did they think the Great Depression skipped the South? I mean, to this day it hurts me to watch anyone throw away a perfectly usable piece of tin foil.

Never mind. The harmless flirting was fun, and I liked the way the attention made me feel.

Thank God for San Francisco. San Francisco was a good training ground for when we moved back to the East Coast and I had to deal with Manhattan. Carroll had moved up high enough on Continental's corporate ladder that they sent him back to New York. Not that we could afford to live in Manhattan, even on his promotion and a big raise. We lived in New Jersey, and he commuted by train. Being a bigwig, he was expected to host bigwig parties, and in turn, a lot of other bigwigs courted his company's business by wining and dining him. I was expected to not only make him look good but also his Wall Street firm. Me, Annie from Virginia.

At least people had been friendly in California. New York, on the other hand, was the center of the universe. It was horrid. I was horrid. I expected the women to be horrid to me. I always needed more than one drink to get ready for those things.

Oh, all right, I can't really say I had a bad time. There's no getting around that it was a glamorous life. Everybody was straight out of fashion magazines, their homes from movie sets. We'd get together and have theme parties and discuss our last European vacation and where to go next. A little bubbly, a martini — any cocktail really — went a long way toward helping me be just the right level of blasé at these functions so I didn't sound too awed by the fact that not only had I been to the Pacific, I had also dipped my toes on the other side of the Atlantic.

May I tell you a secret? It didn't matter. It didn't matter that I had dined in Paris and swam off the island of Crete and golfed in Scotland. Fine, my accent had softened somewhat after San Francisco. But that didn't matter, either. Manhattan was a nightmare, even when there wasn't a party.

The only good thing about moving back East was it brought me closer home and I could visit more often. I had forgotten how pretty Norfolk could be, the little streets that now felt cozy instead of narrow, the old houses no longer domineering but poetic. And it was fun introducing my two little daughters to my birthplace and their people, educating them about Virginia.

Old family friends, Aunt Gee and Uncle Ackie Pennypacker, raised Angus cattle at their small ranch called Spring Hill in Winchester, well north of Norfolk but also well outside Washington, D.C. In the summer, I'd take the girls out of New Jersey on a train south, past the nation's capital and into Virginia, heading for the little village of Winchester to play away our holidays, just like I used to spend my childhood vacations there.

I know you wouldn't think it looking at this wrinkled, papery bodysuit that covers me now, but one summer in Winchester, in my teens somewhere, I was even chosen as one of the Apple Blossom Princesses and rode on a float with the beauty queen of the parade. Swear to God. There's a black-and-white photograph somewhere that would stand witness to this, honey. But I can't even think of where to begin looking for it. You'll simply have to take my word.

Winchester, Virginia, was heaven. Funny how Manhattan made me appreciate a sleepy little town again. The girls got to explore the inside of a house built during the Revolutionary War, and outside there were cows and goats and a pond and space, acres and acres to spare. I got to let my hair down, so to speak, be myself around people I've known my whole life and make them laugh with my caricatures of those supposedly sophisticated folks in the Big Apple. It was a great tonic for me, my annual dose of Southern life. I'd bring those summer memories back carefully wrapped in magnolias in my mind to keep me going through the autumns and winters north.

***

"Nanny?"

"Mom, it's your cigarette dealer. Bobby came with us to visit you today," Carol Anne said, making her voice as light as she could to counter her heavy heart. This might be it. They've been moving her mother around from the nursing home to the hospice to the hospital. Is she ready?

Her son looked around the white hospital room. No more frilly curtains. No more flowery wallpaper. "God, this is depressing," Bob said. "When did you guys move her in here?"

Bob Sr. answered, "Well, she's been having so many mini strokes. They'd bring her to ICU, then her vital signs would stabilize, and they'd move her back to the hospice. But look at the monitor here, Bob, there are barely any brain waves. The hospice just thought it was time."

Carol Anne cleared her throat. "Another thing we need to tell you, Bobby, well, the doctors and the nurses recommended it and we totally agreed — of course, I sent the paperwork to Maggie in Florida and everything — but we've signed the no-resuscitation document. It means, you know ..."

"You all right, Mom? No point in denying reality."

Carol Anne swallowed hard, wiping her eyes. "Still ..."

The young man reached for his maternal grandmother's hand and twined his fingers around hers. "Nanny, I didn't come alone. I've brought someone to meet you. I wish you could see her." He heard his voice cracking as he turned to reach for his girlfriend's hand. "Nanny, I'd like you to meet ..."

cotton balls in ear

name not American

Don't, Anne. Don't black out. Someone might see you and tell on you.

***

"Hi, Mom, it's Carol Anne. Look at you, you're sitting up and everything! How are you feeling? Can you see OK after your eyes being closed for so long? You must be tired of going back and forth between that hospital and here. But you're no quitter! Imagine how surprised I was coming home from work today and there were Maggie and Bob, drinking wine together. She told me that you suddenly opened your eyes and ... woke up! And I said, 'What? After all these weeks? What are we waiting for?' And here we are."

"Momma, it's Maggie. Let me have a hug. Oh, you look just great. The boys send their love, Momma."

"They didn't ..."

Hearing her mother's smoky voice, Carol Anne gasped. "She's talking!" Her eyes welled up.

Maggie touched her mother's back. "Take your time, Momma."

"Your sons didn't — the boys didn't come out with you?"

"Oh, Momma, it's heaven to hear your voice! No. They're very sorry, but it's work and school. They'll try to come out to see y'all real soon. Oh, it's so great to hear your voice, Momma!"

"Florida's a long way, Mom. Maggie's sons can't just drive here like ours can. And look, you've got both your daughters in one place. When was the last time *that* happened?"

"And a son-in-law," Bob Sr. said. "Hi, Nanny. You know who I am? Where's my hug? Oh, that's a good one."

"Where, where are your boys?"

"Oh, school and work," he said. "We told them the good news, though, about your waking up. They're going to come down as soon as they can get away."

"Where they?"

"Bobby's at work still at the *Times'* Orange County bureau. Keith is at USC, Nanny, remember the University of Southern California? You know, in L.A. He's living in the dorm, not with us."

A woman in the other bed in the room had been staring at them all. "This your family, Anne?"

The man turned to face his mother-in-law's roommate. Smiling, he extends a hand. "Hi, I'm Bob. How are you doing?"

It was then that Anne decided to declare, "He's the best son-in-law you could ask for."

Carol Anne's eyes widened. "Aw, Mom." Her voice cracked and her throat tightened.

Bob couldn't believe his ears. "What did she say?"

"Mom told her roommate you're the best son-in-law anyone could ask for."

"Holy crap!"

The roommate grinned proudly at the unexpected gift she had brought into the room.

Bob picked up his mother-in-law's hand as gently as he could. "Thank you, Nanny. That's the nicest thing you've ever said to me."

"And you didn't even have to bribe me."

Carol Anne laughed. "Mom, you want anything to eat or drink? I mean, apple juice maybe?"

But Maggie had other questions. "Momma, what's wrong? Your head hurts?"

Carol Anne suddenly noticed that her mother was leaning her head, way over. "What is she doing?"

"Nanny, are you trying to look at the TV?"

The white-haired woman said simply, "Crank the sound up, will you please?"

Carol Anne turned her head to catch what was on the television behind her. "I don't believe this. Mom, you've been in a coma, and now that you're up and talking we're here to visit you, but you want to watch the Olympics? They're not even playing golf, not even tennis."

"Excuse me." Anne fought her mouth muscles so she could speak with as much dignity and authority as possible. "My mind's not dead yet, you know. I remember that this is the last time the Summer Games are taking place in the same year as the Winter Games. This is momentous. I didn't miss a day of the coverage in February, and as you said, I just came out of a coma. Who knows how long I can keep my eyes open?"

"Hush, Momma, that's all right," Maggie said, rubbing her mother's shoulders. "Don't get excited; it's not good for you. You can do anything you want; you always have." Maggie took the remote and fiddled with the buttons. "There, is that loud enough now?"

"Nanny, do you really remember that the Winter Olympics were in February? You remember where it was?"

"Albertville, of course," the mother-in-law answered the question as if it were beneath her. "You ever make it to France with the Army? Carroll was too old by the time World War II started, thank God."

"No, Nanny. I didn't fight in Europe. I was in Vietnam."

"Oh, that's right. You got married in your uniform and left right after getting Carol Anne pregnant."

"Mom!" Carol Anne laughed at her mother's words.

"And you!" Anne turned, slowly lifting a finger at her youngest daughter. "After he went to war, you came back and lived with us in New Jersey, big as a house and it was fun to watch your body change. A lot more fun than it had been watching *my* body change. You gave birth to Bobby and we sent a wire to the Mekong Delta, wasn't that what it's called?"

"Nanny, you're amazing." (Looking at his wife, Bob asked, "Where did she pull that from?") "The Mekong was where I learned my firstborn was a son, through the Red Cross. Your memory's recovered a lot, Nanny, that's a great sign. What else can you remember? You know where the Summer Games are now?"

"I was just going to ask you. I'm the one who's been in a coma, remember?"

Carol Anne let out one of the whoops that she inherited from her mother.

"Barcelona, Momma," Maggie said. "You're only a day or two behind."

"Mom, the boys are extremely excited because the Olympics opened up men's basketball to all professionals and America is sending the Dream Team: Magic Johnson, Michael Jordan, Larry Bird. Ka-ching! Nobody's gonna beat them."

"Nanny, I bet the boys will come watch the Dream Team with you, offer you a running commentary. You remember what a stud Keith was on his high school basketball team, don't you?"

"What's wrong?" The sudden darkening in her mother's face alarmed Carol Anne. "You don't like that idea? They don't have to come bother you if you don't want them to. Mom, it was just a suggestion."

"Momma?" Maggie squeezed her mother's hand. "Momma, why are you crying?"

***

"Why are you crying?" Indeed. "Why are you crying? Stop that." That's what I said to Keith, and he was what, one year old? Two?

I was at the end of my rope. It had been a long day at Disneyland. Carol Anne, Bob, and I followed Bobby and Keith around from one ride to another. I tried bribing the boys to behave. Mickey Mouse ears and cookies. Keith had such a sweet tooth, just like his mother. I'd make a big production out of hiding a piece of candy in my hand and he'd go, "What tis it what tis it?" "Cat fur to make kitten britches," I'd answer, and they'd laugh and laugh. But that would keep them entertained for only so long. After a while, I just had it with their yammering and whining. I snapped at Keith and spanked little Bob's fanny when he wouldn't stay seated for lunch, and you should have seen the shock on their parents' faces, as if I had tortured the boys or something.

Carol Anne's family was visiting us from where they had settled in Wisconsin. Talk about a backwater outside Milwaukee.

Carroll and I had retired to a little nest right on the edge of a golf course in Fallbrook, just north of San Diego. We found a nice crowd to play golf and tennis with and barbecue with. And because we had done Europe and were now living on the Pacific coast, we started going to Asia on vacations. People in that part of the world might have looked different and the food wasn't always dependable, but the southern humidity sure felt familiar to me.

Carroll was retired. Nonetheless, he handled the insurance for an Episcopalian church nearby, and he was head of the board at the church. He watched over me like a mother hen. He wouldn't hear of anyone saying anything bad about me. Not even after he was diagnosed with lung cancer.

He was a good provider, but it's not as if he was extravagant. I mean, look at my jewelry! I'm not leaving my girls any big rocks or anything, let me tell you. Even so, he took good care of us. He paid for our daughters to go to good schools, too. He used to say, "There are two things for which you shouldn't fret over the costs: an education, and a wedding."

Carroll also used to say that an education is all fine and good, but that a girl needs to learn housekeeping, cooking, and mothering. God knows I was never perfect in his eyes. He was so moody. You could do something, and he'd be pleased as punch, then you do the very same thing the next day and he wouldn't even look at you. Just ask our daughters. He was hard to please, him and his moods.

There was no denying, though, that he was pleased when Maggie surprised us by getting into Duke. I still laugh to think that I had been so relieved to get out of the South yet here my daughter Maggie was moving down to North Carolina. I mean, she did the whole nine yards, cultivating her grades and her Southern accent along real good for a girl born outside San Francisco who went to high school in suburban New Jersey. Married herself a lawyer from North Carolina. And instead of leaving the South like I did, she moved with her husband to Jacksonville, Florida.

Maggie was amazing, I have to say. When we moved back East, she was plump, just entering her teens, and not what you'd call an exceptional beauty or anything, but she had something. Whatever it was, she adapted a lot better than her baby sis and I did. Maggie became a swan. She'd be busy with afterschool clubs and social visits. And Carol Anne, well, Carol Anne would come home crying and complaining that Maggie wouldn't include her in on anything. I learned to have a plate of cookies waiting for Carol Anne so I could have a drink and a smoke in peace. It was our bonding time, though I can't remember what we talked about. Maybe I recited Robert Service, I don't remember. She was asking me how to make friends and why Maggie was so mean to her and not talking to her in school. I didn't know. I had no answer.

How could I have helped her when I didn't know how to help myself? I had no insight, barely any instinct. Maggie, she had both and she wasn't sharing.

Now, see, I'm just thinking too much. It's too quiet in here, and that hospice volunteer's reading voice is just taking over the void. But where is my reader, anyway? Where has everyone gone? Not even a nurse around.

This is where a drink would come in handy 'cause it would drown out the nagging thoughts, those what-ifs and might-have-beens. With a drink or two, you don't need insight, just cling to whatever little instinct you were born with and try not to fall down.

Don't. Don't black out. Someone might catch you. Like Carroll. Or one of your daughters.

Don't parents generally want their children to be better than they were? Or something like that? Carroll and I sent our older daughter to Duke and the younger to the University of Colorado. On school breaks, the older one would get herself invited to long stays in Boston or Atlanta or wherever, any excuse not to come back to — God forbid — New Jersey. The other would come home and just ... she'd just get disgusted with me. Carol Anne never had the decency or the kindness to be tactful. Whatever popped into her head showed up on her face or came out of her mouth. Always caught with her feelings on her sleeve.

I have to admit, though, Carol Anne was useful. And I was grateful. She was old enough by then to drive and go pick up Carroll at the train station in the evenings after his workdays in Manhattan; it gave me time to get myself together before he walked through that door.

Carol Anne was her father's daughter, anyway. Or she tried to act like it. She followed him around and learned to fix things around the house. She even learned how to carve the Thanksgiving turkey.

I didn't know what life held in store for Carol Anne. Maggie knew where she was going and had a general, scheduled plan on how to get there. Maggie took care of herself. Carol Anne didn't want to follow the map you had given her, but it's not as if she were drawing up her own.

That's why when she came home from Colorado that year talking about some fellow university student working as a waiter at her sorority's cafeteria, I wasn't surprised one bit and Carroll wasn't pleased one bit. How did you expect us to react? The boy's family was from Iowa. Dust Bowl people, or they might as well have been as far as we were concerned. It wasn't as if they were anyone Carroll could throw a party for to introduce to his friends and associates. We tried to convince Carol Anne of happiness our way, but when it became obvious she wasn't buying it and insisted on living her life her way, we flew to Denver to meet Bob and the rest of the Elstons, and to make sure he was decent and not a gold digger.

Thank God she was blessed with love. Really, Bob must have loved Carol Anne to put up with us. Let's face it: Carroll and I were far from upset when Bob's family couldn't make it out for the wedding at that pretty little church in Springfield, New Jersey, in 1966. Unlike Maggie's Southern wedding that rivaled royalty, Carol Anne chose a white suit with a simple veil. I got a matching suit in a shade of green because it was near Christmas. I must admit, the groom was impressive in his Army crew cut and uniform. Afterward, we sent them into Manhattan to the Plaza for their honeymoon night. It was what she wanted. It wasn't what he could afford, but it was what she had dreamed of.

I guess for years afterward, we figured that if Carol Anne married for love, she could live on love. We'd help out now and then. When they visited us in California with their kids, Carroll would reimburse them and cover everything while they were with us. But most of the time, we left them alone to live their lives.

Honestly, we thought that was very respectful of us. Not intruding. Carroll and I didn't want to be like our parents, always ready with emotional or financial aid that, of course, would come bound with unwelcomed advice or recrimination. We were of one mind on this, and we accorded Maggie the same respect.

There we were: Three families spread out from California to Wisconsin to Florida. We might as well have been living on three planets. I could have gone on that way forever.

Except they invented secondhand smoke.

They might as well have called me a black widow: She mates, and she kills.

I begged Carroll not to call anybody. I told him I was halfway killing myself anyway and I'd just speed it up so we can go together. But he wouldn't listen to me. I had one of my blackouts and by the time I sobered up, he had sent for help. Up until the day my husband died his horrible, black death, he was taking care of me. He made sure I'd be taken care of after he was gone, though I kept trying to tell him there'd be nothing to take care of after that. What reason would I have left to take another breath, to wake up in the morning? Except for the sensual pleasure of that first sip of alcohol of the day, that first reaffirming inhale of tobacco, Carroll was my only reason to go on living.

And you know, you think you know people. But you don't. I had dismissed Carol Anne and Bob as being pretty predictable. Well, they showed me. They weren't predictable; they were dependable. After Carroll called our daughters to tell them he was dying, it was the youngest and her husband — whom we had treated so shabbily — well, he actually quit his job in Wisconsin and moved his whole family out here so they could take care of me!

And I'm here to tell you, you can't take it back. You can't take failure back. You can say you're sorry you failed someone and try to treat them better. I was taught that's all you can do. But I wasn't ready then to put that lesson into practice. I was so angry Carroll had abandoned me. How do you think that made me feel, Carroll pawning me off as if I were a charity case? I had nothing in common with this youngest daughter of mine and her husband. I wasn't looking forward to their moving out here. I needed a drink just thinking about it.

They couldn't manage it immediately anyway. It took time to sell their house in Wisconsin, and they couldn't just up and leave their jobs. On the other hand, they didn't trust me living by myself. Smokin' and drinkin', and the house didn't have a fire alarm to speak of despite Carroll having been in insurance! A temporary solution had to be found. And that was how "what tis it what tis it" Keith re-entered my life.

***

"Hey, Nanny, can you hear me?"

Keith, now a Phi Delta Theta at USC, asked his mother and aunt, "Is she breathing on her own?" His grandmother was out of the hospice and back in a hospital room.

"Yes," Carol Anne answered, "no more machines. And we signed a no-resuscitation document. But get this! So Maggie and I went through that horrible, heartbreaking decision yesterday and we signed the paperwork. We just, you know, pushed through it. And then that doctor came in today and asked us — out loud, as if we never signed that piece of paper — whether we wanted to keep the machines out of here, basically if we wanted to resuscitate her if her heart stops. God, I mean, don't they have any feelings in this place?"

"Well, probably for legal reasons they're required to ask you face to face."

"Whatever! Fine, I've gotten that off my chest."

"Momma?" Maggie touched her mother's hand. Looking at her nephew, she wished her boys were with her. "What do you think, Keith?"

"Actually," he chuckled, "Nanny looks better than some of the times

I found her unconscious after coming home from school. I mean, she wouldn't have eaten anything at all before she started drinking and she'd look really pasty. I'd just carry her to bed, even though she just reeked of vodka or gin or whatever the drink of the day was."

"The worst was that time Mom fell and actually hit her face on something, right, Keith?" his mom asked. "Those huge purple and ..."

He held up both hands. "I, I — just, let's just not go into it."

Maggie touched his shoulder. "I'm sure it was no fun for a sixteen-year-old boy taking care of his grandmother all by himself all those months. Our family owes you a real debt for taking one for the team, Keith, picking up in the middle of high school and moving out here all by yourself, entering a brand new school and not knowing anybody. You must have been very mature for your age. There was no way either of my boys would have been able to take care of an alcoholic grandmother."

Carol Anne put an arm around her youngest son. "You didn't mind it, did you?"

"Well," Keith said, shrugging.

"I'm sure you were the envy of all your friends," Maggie said. "How many teenage boys get to come and go as they please with no supervision?"

"Actually," Carol Anne said, "I made him phone back to Wisconsin often to give us updates. But he basically got himself to school and fed himself. Didn't you, Keith? He even maintained his straight-A average and was the star of varsity basketball."

"Wouldn't Momma cook?" Maggie asked, then corrected herself. "What am I saying! She hated cooking."

Keith tried to laugh it off. "OK, once in a while there'd be food waiting for me when I got home. Let's just say her housekeeping was lacking."

"Well, it's a testament, Carol Anne, to how you raised him," Maggie said. "You and Bob did a great job parenting. Keith, it's a miracle you weren't tempted to pick up any of her habits. With her passed out, you could have brought all your friends in for a party and who'd be the wiser?"

Keith laughed. "Nanny would give me just enough money for groceries. But I'd challenge you to find any kind of change lying around, not even a penny. It was hilarious. She wouldn't dust, but money, liquor, cigarettes — she was meticulous."

"Mom would tidy all that up, Maggie."

Maggie rolled her eyes. "That's rich! I remember it would drive Daddy up the wall that he was neater than she was. No, you couldn't say she was the typical mother, not exactly apple pie."

"Really?" Carol Anne asked, staring hard into her sister' eyes. "I thought she was all right. She used to make that apricot jam that was just heaven!"

"She fed us and clothed us and took care of us when we were sick. But there's no glossing over the fact that she was, shall we say, workmanlike in her motherhood."

"Really, Maggie? I remember how she could be very comforting."

"Carol Anne, you should absolutely remember her that way. I don't want to take that away from you. And maybe she was a different mother to you. I'm just saying that for me, I couldn't get away fast enough. She was drunk; she was cold. I got more affection from my friends' mothers than from ours. She only really ever loved Daddy. I don't know that she loved herself."

***

You see ... you see what happens when parents try to create a bubble for their children to live in? You see the thanks you get? Granted, I was a demon wrecking our happiness from the inside out, but not that my children ever were supposed to notice. If only I could get back on the ground and look them in the eye, make them hear me, explain that I didn't do anything to them on purpose. They must know before ...

Is that ... is that me down there on that bed, that poor old limp thing? Is that what they're crying over? Can't be. I don't feel lifeless at all. And if that's me there ...

Oh, my girls my girls! Oh!

My girls, if only I could speak to you now.

***

What is it that the more you take, the more you leave behind?

Footsteps. Irreversible, no matter how much you repent the road taken.

I've done enough here, Carroll. May I join you now? Wait for me. I'll be along soon.

*Anne Young died July 31, 1992. She was survived by two daughters, a son-in-law, and four grandsons. To honor her wishes, her family requested the mortuary arrange for her ashes to be scattered at sea.

Three

To be honest, I wasn't looking forward to meeting Nanny that day. It wasn't her. It was me.

More specifically, it was the setting.

My father had died only a year before, on the weekend I turned twenty-five. I was living south of Los Angeles when my mother called to break the news that he was already in a coma at Phoenix Good Samaritan Hospital in Arizona. It's not as if I had never been in a medical ward or had never seen someone dying. I was a police reporter for the *L.A. Times*' Orange County bureau. Even so, I wasn't prepared for the shock of seeing my father, because he was no longer my father.

I don't know how to spare you from having to go through what I did. Chances are that in your lifetime, one of your living grandparents or either your dad or I will end up in the hospital like this, and you, I'm sorry, will hurt and will have to help make end-of-life choices. Please, please, just please remember that none of your elders wants to be a vegetable functioning with no brain control.

The body that used to be my father was hooked up to machines and tubes, including one snaking out of his head to drain the blood from his aneurysm. But his brain and heart no longer housed his soul. The latest medical technology in 1991 couldn't save my father; no amount of family tears could save my father. Your poor grandmother, your Ba, sobbed and signed the release to unhook all life support from her husband, and she and we five siblings gathered around your grandfather's deathbed to say goodbye. I just happened to stand on his right side.

I keep telling myself, even all these years later, that it was an absolute coincidence I was on his right side. Otherwise, how to explain what happened next: We were following Vietnamese death rites. Whoever was standing across from me smoothed over my father's left eyelid. Ba told me, as the oldest, to do the same to his right. I ran my fingers over it, and his eye opened, looking straight at me. I looked at my mother. I closed my father's right eye again, and again it reopened. Ba started to babble something about don't worry, she'll be fine; something about me being his favorite but that I'll be fine; go in peace, she'll be fine. "Thuan, child, you have to tell him yourself or he won't close his eye."

And, though it went against every reason and logic in my head, I heard my voice saying, Dad, please don't worry about me; go in peace. Then I closed his right eye, and it stayed closed.

After that, I ... I never asked my editors not to assign me to funerals or hospitals; I wouldn't dream of admitting such a weakness. I covered crimes and accidents and deaths; I showed up and tried to do my job. If, after interviewing survivors, I sometimes couldn't control myself and had to sob privately in my car, fine, but it didn't mean I could let my mourning stop me from trying to focus on my news assignments.

I didn't want to meet Nanny on her hospital deathbed. By then, your father knew why, but I insisted I must. I followed the Elstons into a room full of machines and tubes. I could hardly breathe. I don't remember anything except Daddy speaking my name, me walking up to his maternal grandmother's bed. I might have said something; I'm not sure. All I remember next is somehow leaving the hospital and lifting my face gratefully toward the sun.

You can understand, don't you, though I didn't want to why I've never regretted going into that room? I needed to see Nanny for myself. At that point, I didn't know anything about Anne Eley, how glamorous and complicated her life was. It didn't matter. I'm sorry to say but at that point, who she was didn't matter to me. The only reason I wanted to see Nanny was that she was a part of Daddy's past and was going to be a part of you, a part of your personal history.

Now I find myself thinking about Anne Eley a lot — how she translated herself into her daughters, who passed their traits onto their sons, and now into you. To help you interpret that inherited personal story, and those of the other great-grandmothers, here's a guide for context.

If, as John Lahr wrote in *The New Yorker*, personal history and public history are "fables agreed upon," then so is language. What's a dictionary except for a set of words and rules that a group of people agreed upon in order to communicate? To translate between two peoples, to understand each other, you need a new set of guidelines to reflect one language in another. See what I mean.

LANGUAGE MIRROR

Vietnamese: English
Viet Nam: Vietnam

Tonal: No accents
Y: Pronounced ee
Nuoc My, My: Beautiful country, America
Hoa Ky: Flower flag (because of the stars), America
Family name before middle and given names: Given name, middle, then family
Nguyen (pronounced win): Smith
Le (pronounced lay): Jones
Tet: Lunar New Year
Ao dai: Traditional long tunic with high collars and split sides, worn over pants

Bo ba ba: Loose button-down shirt (high collar or no collar) and drawstring pants

Ba: A woman, madame, ma'am, Mrs., grandmother

Ong: A man, sir, Mr., grandfather

Noi: Inside, internal

Ngoai: Outside, external

Ong Ngoai: Maternal grandfather

Ba Ngoai: Maternal grandmother

Ong Noi: Paternal grandfather

Ba Noi: Paternal grandmother

Four

NGUYEN, THI KIM
(born March 2, 1921)

"Ba Noi oi, do you know why the year 1861 was important?" the boy asked, muffling his yawn in the thick, humid air of the Ho Chi Minh City night. He didn't want to fall asleep right away, not with his paternal grandmother here. He loved it whenever she stayed over because she told him all sorts of bedtime stories, stories she had memorized from books and from her life, murmured in a crinkly voice that reminded him of the wrinkles on her face. "I bet my daddy that even though you read so much, you can't know everything about that year."

"The French took over Sai Gon," she answered, using the pre-communist name for Ho Chi Minh City. "That's too easy. Silly boy, why are you laughing at me? I'm not mistaken."

"You don't know what else happened in 1861?"

"It could not have been as big as losing the south to the French! Look at how long it took to get it back. But all right, tell me."

"That same year, civil war exploded in America."

"But I thought we were talking about the history of Viet Nam. What are you doing learning the history of America?"

"Slavery, Ba Noi. In fourth grade, we're learning about slavery. My teacher says slavery in America was even worse than how China ruled Viet Nam for a thousand years and how the French colonized us for a hundred years."

"Is that so? You should remember all that to tell your American cousin, show her how smart you are. If you study hard and show her how smart you are, maybe — maybe — one day she might pay for you to go to school in America. And you could maybe even live there."

"Then I will bring you over so you can teach history to my children, like you're teaching me."

"Huh, don't worry. By then, you won't have to worry. There'll be nothing left of me. I'm about to enter history."

In the oppressive night, the boy and his grandmother are lying under a mosquito net on a tenderized bamboo mat spread over a wooden divan. Slowly, she waved a woven straw fan over their faces, closed her eyes, and continued to murmur into his ear. "History is very important. Big or small, old or young, all must learn history. Not understanding history is not understanding the present."

"Yes, Ba Noi," he answered on cue, recognizing the words that will lay down a path for him to follow in the dark, a path down which she has guided him ever since he could talk. He closed his eyes and nestled into his pillow.

"And then, child, remember that whatever you do in the present decides the future. Your future, your children's future. Understand?"

As usual, she didn't wait for his answer but rushed to her next thought. "The problem is that history breeds unintended consequences. History is not destiny, even though you know what happened: when, where, and how. The problem is the why. That's inconvenient. It is inconvenient because in this history of the human race, we humans not only feel too much, we also think too much. We can't help but love and hate, but we also built civilizations around loyalty and betrayal. You think you know which is good or bad, right or wrong. But who are you to judge? That is why knowing the details of a situation is important if you are to understand it. Context will help guide your decisions, especially those hard ones mixed with inconvenient emotions.

"Grandson, believe me when I tell you that when it's your turn, you have to ignore your emotions and let the situation guide you if you want to survive, if you want to leave behind any kind of future for your children and their children. I've sacrificed so much for your father and you, for your aunts and uncles and your cousins. You must remember that, child. Promise?"

"I promise."

***

"When I was born in 1921, Ho Chi Minh was still living in Paris, working as a chef. He had already joined the French Communist Party, but he wasn't Ho Chi Minh yet. He was calling himself Nguyen Ai Quoc-Nguyen being the most common Vietnamese family name, Ai meaning love, and Quoc short for To Quoc, the homeland. What an ideal name for a patriot, right? But that wasn't his real name, either. Does your school teach you this about his story, that he had several names? When he was born in 1890, his parents named him Nguyen Sinh Cung. Grandson, do the math. When he was a baby, it was already three decades after the French takeover of Sai Gon and ..."

"And thirty years after the civil war in America, Ba Noi." The grandson couldn't resist.

"Right, right. We still had seventy more years of French colonization after Ho Chi Minh was born. The French didn't stop there in the south. With the help of their Catholic religion, they began spreading their rule north to where I would enter life.

"In 1932, when I was eleven, Emperor Bao Dai, after being educated for years in France just like his royal elders had been, returned to Viet Nam to ascend the throne. But really that playboy was emperor in title only. Our last king had no power of his own and depended on his French protectors for everything he had, including his life.

"When I turned nineteen and my family started worrying about me becoming an old maid, Germany invaded France. Germany's ally, Japan, then invaded Viet Nam. But instead of taking over the running of our country, the Japanese ordered the French bureaucrats to continue doing their jobs. Can you believe it, child? We Vietnamese were so awed by this other Asian nation being able to order the white men around — these Westerners who had reigned over us for so long — that we assumed the Japanese must have had superpowers, so we let them herd us as if we were cattle.

"And why did the Japanese leave the French that much authority? Who knew? Only the rulers who controlled the guns and bombs and airplanes knew. How could the defenseless common man, woman, or child understand their logic? Who dared ask? But now do you see what I mean when I say history is not black and white?"

She leaned in until her lips felt his ear. "Child, I'm going to tell you something you can't repeat to anyone, not even to your best friend. If anyone else hears this, the security police will come after me for corrupting your mind. Even your closest friend might accidentally tell someone, and it'll get back to your school principal. Can you hear me? I'm whispering because I don't want the neighbors on the other side of the wall to hear. Listen: Don't trust those books they make you read in school. They're all written from the view of a people who had defeated another people. Understand? They don't want you to know how they became the victors; they don't want the books to record history from the view of the people on the other side.

"Though truth be told, it's not just the communist Vietnamese government. In every country, history books get rewritten after every war, after every government takeover. I'm sure it's the same in American schools. Just imagine what books over there say about how America left Viet Nam!"

* * *

The white-haired woman suddenly opened her eyes. "Grandson." She squeezed the boy's arm and, alarmed, he looked at her. "Child, you don't have to ask your cousin about that, American schools and whatnot. It's not polite. You'll remember, won't you?"

He rubbed his eyes. "I don't understand, Ba Noi. Wasn't my cousin born in Viet Nam, too, before her family left? Isn't she Vietnamese?"

"What you say is correct. But your elder cousin grew up in America and learned history in America. Who knows what her schools and her parents have been telling her about Viet Nam, about our family. Child, this is why you have to remember everything I tell you. You have to know my story."

* * *

"In 1941, when I was twenty, Nguyen Ai Quoc sneaked back into Viet Nam and helped create the Viet Minh to fight France and Japan. It was then that he gave himself the name Ho Chi Minh. Three years later, on June 6, U.S. forces washed onto European shores and turned the tides of World War II. The year 1944 was also when Ho Chi Minh gave Vo Nguyen Giap the job of training the Viet Minh military in the jungle. So began the destiny of the French-educated general who would defeat not only the French but also the mighty American war machine. What a hero, that's what school is teaching you, right?

"I ask you, where was this hero, this Mr. General, when the Japanese occupiers forced the French bureaucrats to supply their military? In feeding the Japanese military, the French starved our people. Two million died of famine in the north alone. Have they taught you that? Where were Mr. General and his Viet Minh boy scouts? Where were they when my family couldn't escape starvation? Where were they, I ask you, grandson, when my parents could not escape death, leaving me, already an only child, an orphan?

"And we can't forget Bao Dai, our emperor. What was he doing this whole time on behalf of his subjects? I'll tell you: protecting himself. With the help of his new powerful Japanese friends, Emperor Bao Dai declared Viet Nam's independence from France. But the Japanese didn't stay his friends for long, either. America dropped atomic bombs on the cities of Hiroshima and Nagasaki. That finally vanquished the Japanese. Being vanquished persuaded the warriors of the Land of the Rising Sun to begin sinking back to Japan, handing the Viet Minh the reign of power over Viet Nam. It was then that Bao Dai, the pragmatist, the lover of life and all the women and wine life has to offer, decided to surrender the throne.

"Bao Dai ended the Nguyen dynasty without a fight, and Ho Chi Minh entered the city of Ha Noi on September 2, 1945, as if he were a new king. At a massive public rally, he proclaimed an independent republic of Viet Nam.

"Some independence! Japanese soldiers were still everywhere, and many bureaucracies — such as the Viet Nam Central Bank — were still being run by Frenchmen. I told you: History's inconvenient.

"No, just because America and her Allies won and Germany and Japan surrendered did not mean that the end of World War II brought peace to every corner of the globe. In our corner of Viet Nam, it brought chaos. I bet those schoolbooks of yours don't have even a sentence about how long it took the Japanese to leave. At the same time, the French colonialists weren't going anywhere. In fact, they were waiting for Paris to send more troops. They figured that they had been on the winning side of this epic fight for the universe, and they counted on America to support their right to stay in Southeast Asia.

"Grandson, did you hear what I said? There's no denying that the Americans were already here by then, although only in small numbers. Their mission was to rescue Allied troops whom the Japanese had imprisoned in Viet Nam. But really, they were spies. The first American to die in Viet Nam was killed in 1945, a man in the uniform of a service whose name later magically changed to CIA. How was he killed? What few history books our Vietnamese communist government allows cannot agree about whether it was a misunderstanding or a mistake. But he still was a spy, so I doubt that even American history books tell the truth on that one.

"History books also say that as World War II ended, all sorts of peace negotiations were made over the future of Viet Nam, as well as all sorts of errors of judgment. Everyone and no one accepted responsibility for those errors. The negotiators disagreed, and the war between the Viet Minh and the French officially began in 1946.

"Many people say that war ended in 1954 when General Vo Nguyen Giap's soldiers crushed French forces at Dien Bien Phu. The Geneva Convention divided the country into North Vietnam and South Vietnam. A million northerners fled south, our family among them.

"Many others say the war didn't end until 1975, when the northern communists chased out American troops, took over South Vietnam, and reunified the country back to being just Viet Nam. A million people fled abroad over the next two decades, among them your cousin's family.

"But there are a whole lot of other people who insist that the war has not ended, not as long as this country is still communist, not as long as its flag is still a golden star on a blood-red field.

"That year, 1945, when Ho Chi Minh proclaimed independence from France, was not a milestone just for Viet Nam. Oh, no. That year, my predecessor, Nguyen Thi Nhuan, died at the age of forty-two, leaving four sons. Who was my predecessor? She was the first wife of my husband, the first wife of your Ong Noi."

***

She lowered the fan to her chest, turning her face to the wall.

"Ba Noi?" He gently tugged her sleeve.

"It's late. You have to go to school tomorrow."

"I'm not tired. I want to hear more."

"Enough."

"You've talked about her before."

"Go to sleep."

The bone-thin woman stared into the darkness. It was so noisy here at this son's apartment in the city. There was a constant hum of traffic, mixed with the click-clacks from the night food vendors signaling they were open for business as they meandered from one neighborhood to another. On the other side of the wall, an occasional snort escaped the sleeping neighbors. It was stuffy inside the mosquito netting. Wearily, she flicked the straw fan back and forth over her face. She preferred her quiet neighborhood on the outskirts of Sai Gon, but she was also convinced it was necessary, crucial, to visit with her grandchildren near and far.

So tired, she sighed. So much to prepare before I die. So much left unsaid to the grandchildren, here as well as in America. How can I give all of them the context to make them understand?

***

I was twenty-five, an old maid newly orphaned who did not want to marry. I was living with my mother's sister, and she had a big family of her own. I was just another soul on top of all her worries. My aunt said that in a time of constant war, during which there was a scarcity of non-military work for men, no one was going to give a woman a job — even if my parents had educated me as if I were a son. She said that at my old age, I was lucky to find a position as a wife, for a rich man of status no less. She said I was lucky that my face had a certain elegant beauty to it.

Nguyen Van Hai, seventeen years older than me, was a postmaster in Thanh-Hoa Province.

If you look at a map of Viet Nam, you see it is shaped like an S — a dragon at its full, majestic height, with its head up and its tail bent slightly toward the West. At just where the head of the S ends is where you find Thanh-Hoa.

At the time, being a postmaster didn't simply mean being a bureaucrat. Though we lived under French colonization, the Vietnamese monarchy still ruled, even if in title only. We had an emperor and a mandarin system that dictated caste, taste, and manner. It was a system we inherited from the Chinese, who had dominated us for more than a thousand years before we won independence in 1428, under Emperor Le Loi.

We also inherited their written language, meaning all official communication was in Chinese characters. Our spoken language was a mixture of Chinese and regional dialects. In the 17th century, French missionary Alexandre de Rhodes completed the transcription of Vietnamese speech into a written language, using the Roman alphabet. But this written Vietnamese was considered base and unacceptable by the elite. You weren't educated and cultured unless you could write in Chinese ideographs.

In a strange way, the mandarin system was democratic. If you weren't born into a family with status, you didn't have to stay outside forever looking in. Any man could study hard then try to become a mandarin by taking a civil service test given every few years at the Temple of Literature in Ha Noi.

On examination day, rows and rows of scholars in their best caps and gowns would be kneeling at their desks in the temple courtyard, sons of farmers and tradesmen right alongside those of governors and judges. The exam covered history, law, math, and science, but it leaned heavily toward ancient text and literature. It had a lot to do with reciting by memory, but you also had to be quick on your feet. Each scholar was given lines of poetry newly written by the king or some other member of the royal family, and each contestant would have to respond on the spot with a poem of his own. You were graded for both the rhyme and the reason behind your response, even on how noble your thought was.

If you passed the examination, you won glory and silk and gold, and you were assigned some civil service posting. Depending on how you scored, the palace could send you out as a governor, judge, prosecutor, postmaster, and so on, and your family would be taken care of for life. If you failed the exam, it would be only a temporary shame, then you had a few years to recover to try again at the next open imperial contest of the brain.

The French did not change this system much after they began colonizing Viet Nam. Why should they? It provided a steady stream of Vietnamese mandarins who helped maintain the order that kept the French in control. Nonetheless, you had to hand it to the Vietnamese. Even in our humiliation of being a dominated people, we took what we could get. The Vietnamese have always been very practical, adaptable people. Whatever helped us not only to survive but also to get ahead, we learned it, practiced it, then perfected it.

You want to hear about unintended consequences? Among the Vietnamese elite, some were even more French than the French. Others would take what they learned and use it against France.

What irony. If we as a nation were honest, we must face the fact that we had brought French colonization on ourselves. Well, Nguyen Anh did; he thought he could use the foreigners and control them. A survivor of a clan that ruled southern Viet Nam, Nguyen Anh was vying against other regional chieftains for the top job, to rule over the whole nation. He listened to a French Catholic priest and sought help from France. Nguyen Anh sent his seven-year-old son with this priest to Versailles in 1787, and the boy so charmed Louis XVI and Queen Marie Antoinette with his exotic dress and precociousness, they made him a playmate for their son. With military and financial support from France, the Nguyen dynasty would reign over Viet Nam for more than a century, ending with Bao Dai, an emperor who would be used and controlled by foreigners.

Over those hundred-plus years, the Nguyens sent their princes to France for an education and their princesses for finishing school. Imitating the imperial family, Viet Nam's elite also sent their sons and daughters abroad, or to the best schools at home run by foreign missionaries. There was no getting around the fact that knowing Chinese and French, not to mention the new written Vietnamese once it was transcribed into the Western alphabet, enhanced your chance of gaining status and riches. After the French weakened the Nguyen monarchy and began their colonization in the 1860s, you really couldn't become a mandarin unless you knew all three languages. The French occupiers needed the mandarins to help them run the country, and this system continued into the twentieth century.

My husband was a mandarin, and he had some money that went with his status. His sons — already in their teens by the time I joined the family — learned all three languages and were expected to be familiar with all three cultures.

From what I saw, however new in my job as a wife to him and stepmother to his sons, my husband barely worked. He supervised at the French colonial post office. The rest of the time, he played cards. Playing cards was so ubiquitous in our house, sons and servants picked up the skill.

***

I picked up a skill, too, a very practical one: giving birth. I learned it and perfected it. To his brood of four sons, I added four more sons and four daughters.

***

Ask any mother what she would not do for her children. Mine changed my life. They were not his. They were mine. And nothing else mattered except their well-being. Once I became a mother, my education and my obsession with history transformed from the abstract to the practical: How could I use all I knew to ensure the survival of my children and their children?

And, you see, the proof is in my grandchildren! I often look at them and can't believe what we had to do to save the future from the past, over and over.

Once the Viet Minh began their quest to end colonization, their hunt for anyone who worked for the French became so intense that my husband had to change his name from Nguyen Van Hai to Le Tat Tien. In 1954, we escaped communist North Vietnam and started over with nothing in South Vietnam. When my husband died in 1971, yet another life began. Four years later, after South Vietnam was no more, my children and I had to rebuild our lives again, under the reunified, communist Viet Nam. Through all those years, everything I ever did was for my children.

Some would accuse me of being selfish. But I was selfless in my selfishness. You can't judge me without knowing my past. You have to know who I am.

***

Nguyen Thi Kim, 73, seated at a banquet table with family and friends, smoothed her brown embroidered ao dai over her legs and looked around the open-air restaurant. It was night, but it might as well have been day because of the harsh streetlamps and the gentle fairy lights hanging over the courtyard. Raising a hand to check the coiled white hair at the nape of her neck, she looked down at her plate full of garlic crab claws and ginger chicken wings. What to do? Should she use her fingers in front of the foreigners?

In the spring of 1994, after the communist regime in Ha Noi opened its doors to economic change, U.S. President Bill Clinton lifted the trade embargo Washington had imposed at the end of the war. As if awakened from oversleeping, Viet Nam rushed to make up for the two lost decades. From north to south, abandoned buildings and rice paddies turned into a modern money crop: development, construction sites that transformed the drab landscape into glass high-rises, spa hotels, and garden villas. As the number of jobs increased, lives improved. People renovated their homes, improved their diets, and sent their children to better schools. On the streets, motorcycles gradually outnumbered bicycles. More foreigners started visiting and then staying — from all over, not just from Russia and the countries that used to make up the Soviet Union before it broke up in 1991.

Now it was autumn 1995, and Madame Kim found herself sitting at a new restaurant in a new Ho Chi Minh City she hardly recognized. What was the occasion? Granddaughter Thuan had returned to live in her birthplace for a while. Partly because Thuan was both Vietnamese and American, she had found a job with a joint venture developing golf resorts. She did not come back alone. With her was a young American named Bob who was taking Vietnamese classes at Ho Chi Minh City University and teaching English to Asian business executives. They had been married in California, but they were having a second wedding reception tonight for the Vietnamese relatives. And Madame Kim, dressed in her best ao dai and introduced to Thuan's foreign friends and co-workers, couldn't help but be proud to have an American granddaughter.

Though technically, Thuan was not of Madame Kim's blood. Thuan's father, Nghia, was one of the four sons from the predecessor:

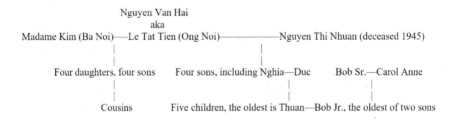

Nguyen Van Hai
aka
Madame Kim (Ba Noi)—Le Tat Tien (Ong Noi)——————Nguyen Thi Nhuan (deceased 1945)

Four daughters, four sons   Four sons, including Nghia—Duc   Bob Sr.—Carol Anne

Cousins   Five children, the oldest is Thuan—Bob Jr., the oldest of two sons

***

"Mother, the car is here."

"Is tea ready?"

"Thuan is bringing Bob here for the first time. I've ordered Coca-Colas."

My youngest son, so considerate. Thinh was studying English and computer something or other at a tech school nearby, and when he wasn't studying, he helped me with the cooking and cleaning. My oldest son was another matter. He was a handsome man, but there was something wrong with his mind. No concentration; he had never been able to hold down a job. My two other sons tried to do what they could, but they had their own families to worry about.

Of course, my four daughters had done all the housework when they were alive. Well, one was still alive, but she was ill. She had been ill for a while.

We used to have a maid. After Sai Gon was "liberated" in 1975, we learned that the maid had been a Viet Cong cadre all along. We thought she had used her day off once a month to visit family, but she was actually attending communist meetings and was spying on us and the neighbors. I heard that she now had a desk job down at the Ho Chi Minh City People's Committee, in a building that took up an entire block. Before '75, it was the City Hall of Sai Gon. The French constructed it in the early 1900s and modeled it after the Hotel de Ville in Paris, in what Westerners call the "gingerbread house style."

Comical, wasn't it? My former maid got to dress up every day in a silk ao dai to work at a government job in a beautiful, ornate building painted bright yellow and white. And I, in my cotton bo ba ba, got to sit here all day, mistress of a narrow house that hadn't been painted in a long time. Just look at that metal front gate rising all the way to the ceiling, the dull cement floor, the front room where we parked our bicycle and motorcycle, and then this sitting room. It wasn't much: a red, plastic sofa set; an electric fan; a glossy calendar from some foreign company tacked onto the wall; the family altar with photos of our ancestors, my husband, and children of ours who had died young. Thuan's father had not been as young as the others; Nghia had passed away at the age of fifty-eight in America, just several years ago.

At least Thinh dusted the altar and refilled the incense bowl. If Thuan wanted to pray to the ancestors later, at least she'd find new grains of rice to hold up the incense sticks.

Thinh opened the gate and I heard, "Ba Noi oi."

"Granddaughter, enter."

Thuan appeared with her giant husband and walked quickly toward me. She touched my shoulder as she sat down. "Ba, are you well?" She handed me a bouquet of flowers. "We've brought these as an offering for the altar."

"Oh, what fragrance. Thank you, granddaughter. Thinh, son, find a vase." I didn't know whom to examine first, Thuan or this tall, pale man behind her. My sons had warned me that this grandson-in-law might unintentionally show disrespect by visiting me in what they call the American uniform: T-shirt and long shorts that look like pajamas. But Thuan must have instructed her husband because he was wearing a button-down shirt and long pants. The poor American; we didn't have air conditioning.

The giant smiled at me and opened his mouth, "Chao Ba."

"Oh!" Heaven and earth. "*Hao a u*? Granddaughter, did I say that correctly? If your husband's taking the trouble to learn Vietnamese, I should try speaking English."

The young American smiled at me and spoke in Vietnamese again, "You speak good behavior."

"Ha ha ha ha ha. But that's all right. I understood you. Sit, sit down. Granddaughter, tell your husband to sit down. Uncle Thinh will get you some cold sodas."

"Oh no, Uncle. We can drink tea."

Thinh, putting the vase with Thuan's flowers on the altar, spoke as if we bought sodas every day. "It's too hot. The shop is just next door. I've already told them to put two cans on ice."

As he left, Thuan asked again, "Ba, are you well?"

"Oh, the town of Thu Duc is so dusty now. It's as bad as Ho Chi

Minh City, everywhere motorcycles and smog. At least your company gave you a car."

"Yes, Ba. And the driver's a good man. He speaks Vietnamese slowly to my husband and teaches him new vocabulary. My husband likes learning the local slang. I'm learning, too!"

"Do you have to pay the driver?"

"The company pays, Ba."

"How much a month?"

"One hundred thirty U.S. dollars."

"One hundred thirty American dollars is almost ... two million Viet Nam dong! Your driver's family must be very grateful." Oh Heaven, if your uncle could drive for you, I would also be very grateful! This crazy new economy ... even if Thinh got a computer job, it's not certain he'd get paid as much as a driver for a foreign company. Sigh, he's back. Should I tell him?

"Coca-Colas all right? Now that there's no more trade embargo, American products have flooded the market. I just read in the newspaper about the intense competition between Coke and Pepsi."

"Oh, Uncle, the war between the two companies is insane. They're battling for global domination. They both have offices here now, and they're bidding against each other to sponsor a golf tournament at my company's resorts. Aren't you drinking Coke, Uncle? It's too much sugar soda for just the two of us."

"It's all right. I want to save my appetite for dinner."

"Does your husband like Viet Nam?"

"Very much, Ba. Bob has lived several summers in China and Taiwan, studying Mandarin and teaching English, so this is nothing new to him. He likes living in Asia."

"If your father were alive, he'd speak Mandarin with your husband." I turned to look into the American's light eyes and enunciated slowly: "Thuan's father, aside from Vietnamese, knew Chinese, French, and English." I patted her arm. "Let your husband know that your father was very smart."

She spoke to him, chuckling, then he answered in several long sentences, smiling at me.

"Ba Noi, my husband wants me to tell you that his father was a soldier in Long An, down in the Mekong Delta. My father-in-law was a soldier in Viet Nam when my husband was born in America, so as a baby, my husband lived with his mother at her parents' house."

"Really? Does Bob know that when you were born, your father was also at the front? Both fathers were fighting on the same side and — just think — you also lived with your mother's family until your father came home. What does Bob call his grandparents on both sides?"

"Ba, in English there's no Noi or Ngoai. Generally speaking, it's just Ba, *Grandmother,* or Ong, *Grandfather.*"

No inside or outside? Well, that made sense. It was America, new world, new future. No ancient terms and titles that came down through the centuries-old domination by the Chinese and their Confucian traditions. The family used to be everything, its support system the social net. A family's sons married and would bring their wives back to live in the family home. A family's daughters married and would move out to live with their husbands' side. As each child was born, he learned to call the grandparents living in the same house with him, his father's parents, his inside grandparents — Ong Noi, Ba Noi. When he visited his mother's parents, he called them his outside grandparents — Ong Ngoai, Ba Ngoai.

That tradition still existed when Thuan was born in 1966, whether her mother liked it or not. How could Duc, that hard-headed woman, live with me, or with any mother-in-law?

I was lucky that when I joined my husband's clan (it must have been 1948), we didn't live with his family and only had to pay respect once in a while at the ancestral village, which took days to get to by boat and several hours even by the French automobile. My husband was from Thuong-Tu Village in Thai-Binh Province, out in the north. At the front of the house where he was born, there was a pond where my stepsons used to take my little children swimming. Inside the red-roofed, stone home, there were shelves and shelves of books collected by my father-in-law, a widower, scholar, and herbal healer.

"Has your mother told you that your great-grandfather's house is still there in the province of Thai-Binh? I've been exchanging letters with relatives in the north."

"Yes, Ba Noi. In America, my mother gets letters from them, too. Now that I'm back living in Viet Nam, she wants me to go up there to visit all these old ancestral homes and meet my distant cousins."

"Your paternal great-grandfather, my father-in-law, had lost his wife very early, probably through childbirth. He loved all his grandchildren, but especially your dad. Wherever the old gentleman went, your dad followed. It was your great-grandfather who nicknamed your dad 'Knowing Mind' because he was so smart. Your dad learned to read by reading my father-in-law's books."

"Really, Ba?" Thuan smiled, tears in her eyes. "I wish that when my father was alive, I had asked him more questions about his childhood."

"I wasn't there when your father was a child. But I have heard the story of when your father was very little and visiting the ancestral village, he'd wake up from naps crying out for his grandfather. And the old gentleman would come in asking, 'Who's sitting there like a pile of manure?' Then he'd lift up the mosquito netting, and your dad would plunge into his arms and laugh out loud. Yes, your great-grandfather truly adored your father. When the old gentleman died, your dad was nearly a young man. Our family already had gone through so much."

"What year was it, Ba? What had you gone through?"

"Oh, never mind. It's too sad. It would take too much time. Light some incense for your ancestors, let them know you've come home."

Thuan stood, and I was impressed that though she was raised in America, she knew what to do: Light three joss sticks, bow in front of the altar, and plant the incense into the rice bowl. While her husband followed her example, she looked at all the framed photographs and said, "It's so sad, Ba. When I left Viet Nam, all four of my aunts were alive. Now there's only one."

"How old were you?"

"I was nearly nine. We left a week before Sai Gon was lost."

"That's right, you left with your mother's whole family. Even your Ba Ngoai made it to America, and she's older than me. I wish I had listened to your father when he came around that night, giving us a chance to come along. But your young uncles said, 'Really, how bad can the new government be? They might be communists, but we're all still Vietnamese together.' Your uncles didn't listen to me. Your father was smart. He remembered history. Your father remembered the hardship of those last years in Ha Noi before our family escaped in 1954. Thanks to your father's decision to go to America, you live happy lives. Here, all our suffering is because I listened to your uncles and we stayed!"

"Ba Noi, which of my aunts died first?"

"Your aunts are leaving the world in the same order they came in. Strange, isn't it? Tuberculosis hit all four girls and spared all four boys."

"My youngest aunt has tuberculosis, too? I didn't know."

"She's taking medicine."

"Oh, I should go visit her. I'm so bad." Thuan shook her head. "I've been so bad. I'm still learning this sales job, and I just haven't had the time."

"You should telephone first. She's not as pretty as once upon a time. All that medicine makes her all puffy. You remember her nature, shy and quiet. Now, she rarely meets with outsiders."

"No wonder she didn't come to our wedding party. That night, when I saw only Uncle and their children, I had wondered what's wrong."

What are you insinuating? "At the reception, did you see that your aunt's daughter looked exactly like her? She's so pretty; she's almost a maiden. And your aunt's sons, oh, they're so smart. They're all doing well in school." You see, everything's normal. No one's to blame. You can't blame me for everything that's happened. Ask yourself: If you were me, what would you have done?

Missy, you have to understand my situation at the time. Only one of my four daughters had managed to find a husband, the oldest one, but she was also the first to get tuberculosis. She couldn't have kids.

Her husband was a handsome, talented man, a photographer with his own business. He wanted children to carry on his line. I had to think of a way. By then, the next two daughters already were sick. But the youngest one, the prettiest one, was still healthy. He loved his wife, but he's a rational man who saw my logic. He agonized over my request, but he finally agreed. Well, yes, my oldest was not happy. But they lived under one roof for just a while, until the older one died. Her husband got three children, she died with no shame of divorce, and her youngest sister gained a haven for life. What more do you want?

Missy, people who didn't have to live through reunification just don't understand. Did you think a stable life was easy to come by after the communists took over Sai Gon? You couldn't go to school or get a job unless your family had been among the revolutionaries because — as they preached constantly to the rest of us — only *they* had earned the right to the good life because *they* had fought to liberate the rest of us from France and America.

But truth be told, even the revolutionary families had a rough time right after '75. We were an isolated country punished by economic embargoes, no foreign investment. The Soviets couldn't help much. They only had enough to keep up the façade of their communist empire.

Thank Heaven and Buddha that a few years after '75, the Ha Noi regime allowed us to contact our relatives abroad for help. How could we have lived these two decades without the gift money and the cartons of supplies your family sent back from America every year?

Who's touching me? Let go of my arm!

"Ba Noi, what's wrong? I just want to take my husband out back. I remember playing in the yard and having so much fun."

"Ah." Breathe in, breathe out. Calm down. "It's not as green as it used to be, but all right."

They might as well see how we really lived in this narrow house — this sitting room, right behind it the one bedroom that backed into the kitchen. There was never enough money left over to fix up anything around here. Look, we still have an outhouse! Let her see I'm not stashing away any wealth.

Thuan followed me into the yard. She looked up at her husband. *"It's ... brown. I remembered it being green. This is a lot smaller than I remembered, too."*

Who knew what she was saying about me. I needed to get out of this sun. "Let's go back inside. It's too hot out here."

She followed me, saying, "Ba Noi, do you go back to your old house in Sai Gon at all? I took my husband to train crossing No. 6 last week to show him where I lived when I was tiny."

"It's a coffee shop now."

"Yes, we took pictures of me in front and it smelled so good, all those beans in the jars they displayed right in the window."

"Did you go see your Ba Ngoai's house, too? At least your mother's siblings were able to sell it before they went to America."

"Yes, from your old home I followed the train tracks down to Ba Ngoai's place on the left. So sad, Ba Noi! The new owners have turned the sitting room into a motorbike shop, but the cotton tree is still out front. The house is a lot smaller than I remembered. It used to have such nice furniture, but it's black and greasy now."

After Thuan was born in 1966, Duc brought her straight from the hospital to live at her mother's house because Nghia was still at war. Soon, though, he left the military. Nghia said that after holding his baby daughter, he didn't want to risk having her grow up without a father. He was always the emotional one, unlike his wife. Once Nghia no longer was in the military, he brought Duc and Thuan home to live with us. I knew Duc didn't like it any, the independent woman she was. When she got pregnant with the second one, they made excuses about not wanting to be troublesome and moved out.

"To your eyes, granddaughter, everything must look smaller after you've been used to tall houses and wide doors in America. The pictures your father mailed us were amazing. Four bedrooms and two bathrooms for only your parents and the five of you children!"

"Ba Noi, when did you move here to Thu Duc?" she asked, sitting back down and sipping her Coke. "I just remember that it was before we left in '75. I was what, eight or nine years old? The first time we visited Thu Duc from Sai Gon, it seemed so far. And now it takes only a half-hour. In America, Ba, it took longer than that for me to drive to the university."

I knew it. Now we would learn the real reason why Thuan and her giant husband were visiting me. "Yes, several years after your grandfather died, I sold the house in town and moved out here. Thu Duc was like the countryside then, and quieter, the air better for your aunts' tuberculosis."

"I remember that my house and my school in Sai Gon were all cement and concrete. But visiting you out here, I was amazed to see an actual yard with grass that we ran around in. And you had chickens." Thuan giggled.

"All gone. No more. The fruit trees died, and I had to sell the chickens. You have to understand that after reunification, we lost everything. We couldn't even eat those chickens ourselves. You're lucky you didn't have to suffer, thanks to your father's decision to fly away."

So, Miss America, don't ask for that money back. The proceeds from the sale of the Sai Gon property were long gone. You thought treating four daughters with tuberculosis was cheap? And on top of it, trying to make something of my four sons — bribes to get them into the right schools, paying for weddings they wouldn't be ashamed of in front of their new in-laws. My sons had never ridden new motorcycles to work. Even now, Thinh only had a bicycle to take him to university.

I knew Thuan's mother sent her here for a purpose. Duc had never forgiven me for not sharing the money from the sale of our house in Sai Gon. Duc thought I cheated my stepchildren out of their inheritance and kept everything for my own children. What had she been telling Thuan?

I didn't know whether Thuan still remembered everyone arguing over the word "stepmother." Thuan had just learned to read, and on her visits, that little girl would show off to her aunts and uncles. Nghia had bought his firstborn all the translated Western fairy tales — Snow White, the Little Cinder Girl. One of my sons asked Thuan what she thought of stepmothers. And she answered, with no hesitation and with a big nod, that stepmothers were wicked witches. Of course we told Nghia about it when he came to pick her up, and of course he apologized that Thuan was just talking about the books. But who could believe that Duc didn't talk ugly about me?

After that, I hardly spoke to Thuan's mother. And when I sold the house in town, Duc hardly spoke to me. Anyway, Nghia was some big editor at an English-language weekly newspaper. He told me he didn't need the money and to keep it for all his younger siblings.

What a good man. Oh, why did Nghia have to die so suddenly? "Your poor father; fifty-eight was too young. Your Ong Noi didn't even get a stroke until his sixties. If your father only lived on just two, three more years, he could have come back to Viet Nam with you."

"Ba Noi, you don't have to worry."

"Worry what?"

"My mother made a promise at my father's deathbed that even though he's gone, she'll continue to help you as much as she can while she's still alive. My father knew his responsibility to you and the family; my mother tells us children all the time that he worried about you. I'm living here for a while now, so I'll come when I can."

"Your mother tells you that?"

"Don't worry, Ba Noi, nothing will change. My husband and I have to go now, but this is for my cousins." Thuan pressed an envelope into my hands.

"What is this?"

"I don't know who needs more money than others. Please, you divide it out for me. You know who needs what. School fees, books, new clothes. It's a lot of expenses. Let me help my little cousins. And please give some to Uncle Thinh. I don't want to hurt his pride, his niece offering him money, but I'm sure he has expenses."

"Yes, I thank you, granddaughter. Uncle Thinh's a good son. And he's studying hard and hopes to get a good job. If you hear of any job opening at your company, remember to let him know?"

"Yes, Ba. Uncle?"

Thinh descended from the attic: *"You are leaving? I was studying."*

Hearing the English words, the American looked up. *"Hey, Uncle Thinh, your accent's very good. My Vietnamese is still so bad. If you want, we can help each other out."*

"That is a good plan, Bob. Thank you. Niece, your husband is so nice."

"I thank you, Uncle." Thuan grinned at him then looked at her husband. *"Bob, say, 'Chao Ba.'"*

The giant bowed his head to me. "Chao Ba."

"I'll be back, Ba Noi. Oh, my husband wanted me to tell you that his parents will be visiting us soon here. It will be his father's first time back to Viet Nam since the war. We'll bring them here to pay their respects."

"Yes, yes. I won't forget your words." Your mother made a promise?

***

Madame Kim watched her Vietnamese American granddaughter disappear out of the metal wall gate. The hollow-cheeked woman rubbed her watery eyes, Thuan's words echoing in her ears.

Promises and vows. Vows and promises. Her surprise that Thuan's mother would make such a promise wilted, and an anger bloomed in its place. After all, Madame Kim thought, it's not as if my husband kept his vows.

Picture this: His first wife, Madame Nhuan, was ill in Thanh-Hoa Province in the north. With what, nobody knew. When you got sick back then, you were just sick. We didn't know about cancer or tuberculosis or anything like that. But it was serious, he told me later. He had put Madame Nhuan and their four sons on a boat down the Red River Delta to her native village, where her family hoped to nurse her back to health. He told me that as he put her on the boat, she made him promise to take care of their boys. She understood he'd have to remarry, but he must take care of his sons. And he promised. Madame Nhuan never made it back to her village. She died along the way, and they had to pull the boat over to bury her on a nearby island. Her four boys watched her die; the mandarin wasn't there because he had stayed in Thanh-Hoa in his big house with his big job.

Toward the end of his life, my husband remembered all sorts of things and wanted to get them off his chest. All his guilt, he dumped on my head. He recounted how, a few years after we had been married, we were on a boat trip that took us past the island where my predecessor was buried. He had promised his sons he'd take them to visit their mother's grave. But I was pregnant, again. I told him I was not feeling well and had to get back to our house as quickly as possible. I told him it was either the dead grave or the live soul growing inside me. My husband told the boat owner to take us home. But how was that my fault? He was the one who broke the promise to his sons, not me. Yet he had the audacity on his deathbed to make me promise to share the money from the sale of the house in Sai Gon! As if I owed him, or his sons, anything.

The bone-thin, white-haired woman felt her face flushing and her pulse racing. She leaned back on the plastic sofa, closed her eyes, and envisioned the Vietnamese American granddaughter sitting next to her. She tried to slow her breathing.

Granddaughter, there was one day you were visiting us with your parents. Ong Noi was sixty-six, after the stroke ... you fed him soft-steamed peanuts, and he was smiling and drooling like a baby. Your parents were boasting you'd be starting kindergarten soon. It was that night or maybe a few nights later, I was getting Ong Noi ready for bed when he gripped my hand, and I knew it was the death grip. Just think, if it were you, how would you feel? All those years together and now at the end, he didn't even say my name. He didn't thank me for wiping his butt and treating his bed sores those last months. He just gripped my hand and said, "Divide evenly."

I am not a cruel person. You have to understand that this will happen to you and Bob, too. Just wait and see. Ong Noi had ceased to be my husband, and I already was making lists of what must be done. I had his funeral to organize and my children's future to think about. I shushed him and stroked his cheek until he closed his eyes.

Le Tat Tien passed away on March 30, 1971. I turned the page on that chapter and began my fifties.

to be continued

Five

April 30, 1975

On a U.S. military base in Guam, in a Quonset hut my family had shared with two dozen other families since we fled South Vietnam a week before, the bunk beds were filled with people listening to my father translate a BBC radio announcement: Saigon, our nation's capital, had fallen to northern communists.

No one made a sound. Not even a gasp. Then a child started sobbing. Dad said, "Maybe the adults have no more tears."

The spell broke. While some stayed in their beds and stared into space, others drifted outside toward the cafeteria that by then was serving 20,000 refugees. It was lunchtime, after all. What else was there to say? Everyone was exhausted. As a song sums up Vietnamese history until then: A thousand years enslaved by the Chinese enemy; a hundred years dominated by the French; 20 years of daily civil war — a mother's legacy I leave for you.

For the Vietnamese on both sides of the civil war, more than 4 million soldiers and civilians had been killed or wounded, ten percent of the population.

Of the 3 million servicemembers Washington sent to South Vietnam, nearly 60,000 had died and 150,000 had been wounded, including my future father-in-law.

The last U.S. combat troops left in 1973, but American diplomats, security units, and journalists stayed till the end. My father, a former South Vietnamese lieutenant fluent in several languages, was managing editor of an English-language weekly, *The Vietnam Sun*. He told my mother to begin preparations to flee. In his youth in the north, Dad had wanted to join the nationalist Viet Minh to end French colonialization, but when it turned communist, he lost all illusions. Both his and Mom's families abandoned homes and businesses in 1954 because they didn't want to live under communism. My parents now realized they'd have to do it again.

By 1975, I was in third grade, the eldest of five. South Vietnam's president resigned on April 21. Early the next morning, packed with family photos, a change of clothing for each of us, and all of $20 U.S., my parents took us kids in a taxi to the airport. We spent all day standing in line, unsure whether we'd be leaving that day or would have to return home and try again tomorrow. About nine that night, we were among dozens of families who boarded a U.S. military cargo plane. For the adults, stressed and scared about the unknown, the departure was utter war trauma. For the children who had never been on an airplane, it was a total adventure. After our C-130 was in the air, American soldiers went around shining flashlights out the windows. When Dad asked why, they said that we had been shot at, but that the darkness helped so only the wings were nicked.

We spent that night at a U.S. military base in Manila, the Philippines, sleeping on single military green air mattresses with thousands of other refugees. Then we spent a week in Guam and a month north of San Diego at Camp Pendleton, one of several bases assigned refugee duty on the U.S. mainland.

When we arrived that May, Camp Pendleton had 18,000 Vietnamese living in eight "tent cities," including my maternal grandmother, most of her children, and their children. One of my cousins was even born there; his parents named him Ky, short for flag and America, *Hoa Ky*. My parents and five kids were assigned to city No. 8, tent 88, which we shared with several other families. By the time the operation closed five months later, Camp Pendleton had aided more than 50,000 refugees.

We were among a million Vietnamese who fled over the two decades after the war ended, an unprecedented exodus for a time of peace. Hundreds of thousands, labeled "boat people," heroically chose to confront the perils of the open sea in never-big-enough boats — and risked raping, pillaging, and killing by pirates — rather than stay in Vietnam. Those who survived lived for years, some for decades, in refugee camps in Southeast Asia before being sponsored to new homes.

The world determined that the "boat people" were an emergency crisis in the 1980s. But we didn't anticipate al-Qaeda or the medieval barbarity of terrorists who would sacrilegiously call themselves the Islamic State. Children would live in refugee camps again. Four decades after the Vietnam War, with tens of millions of people displaced because of conflict or persecution in Afghanistan, Iraq, Somalia, Syria, Yemen, and elsewhere, the world would witness its largest refugee crisis since World War II. To this day, looking at photos of kids staring out of a refugee tent, I can't turn away. I still see myself in their eyes.

***

My brothers just flew back to the West Coast after visiting us for Thanksgiving. The bachelor shared the boys' room and reported that my two youngest children had talked in their sleep.

Neither of you remembered what you had been dreaming about. You weren't old enough yet for me to teach you to still your waking consciousness for a few seconds so it could coexist with your receding subconscious, so you could see your dream before it faded.

Just this morning, I woke up pleased to envision my name in marketing material for a couple of critically acclaimed artists whom I had discovered. Then the sun shone on my husband sitting up beside me in bed, and I realized my artists had been a dream.

Not all my dreams were such *Vanity Fair*. There was one of me on a road trip: It's night; I need to fill up the tank. But on this freeway, they must be testing some next-generation gas stations because everything's flat on the ground, and I can't figure out how to use any of it.

Other dreams had me living in a cave, or sharing a room of crowded beds, or walking from my resort to the beach. In some dreams, I was with Daddy, in others, with you; sometimes I was with all of my children. There was one that kept returning: I'm wandering winding alleys looking for my favorite noodle restaurant in Vietnam. I found it once, and next time I see you in a dream of my birthplace, I'll take you there.

Most of my mornings were like that, waking up with my head still part of whatever world I had been living in my sleep. I discussed this hypothesis with you kids, how some of my dreams were so vivid and so detailed, I thought they were my other lives. Maybe sleep gave me a glimpse into my alternative selves, different destinies. Can you have more than one destiny?

Jorge Luis Borges asked in *The Garden of Forking Paths*: When a man faced several alternatives in life, what if instead of choosing one and eliminating the others, he chose all? He'd then create what Borges called diverse futures and diverse times, which also would multiply and fork.

Think about that. In some of those diverse times, my family must not have escaped to America! How would I have met your dad? If I hadn't, you children wouldn't have been born, carrying my bloodline and his. I shuddered to even imagine another dimension without you. But there was a physicist named David Deutsch who believed in multiple universes; he wrote books titled *The Beginning of Infinity* and *The Fabric of Reality*. At Oxford's Center for Quantum Computation, Deutsch tried to build a computer to test for the existence of those multiple universes. What if, in a parallel life, he succeeded?

I learned the possibility of other lives and universes through the Buddhism philosophy of karma and reincarnation that played a major role in my upbringing, even in Arizona.

In the summer of 1975, after spending a month at the Camp Pendleton refugee camp, my family was sponsored to Phoenix by the Mount of Olives Lutheran Church. To show our thanks, my dad decided we should get baptized. As my mom used to say: All true religions teach you to be good; that can't be bad. We went to church every Sunday. My siblings and I participated in many church activities — Sunday school, chorus, handbell choir, and confirmation.

Other churches had also sponsored many of my mother's siblings and their families to the Valley of the Sun. Several years later, the refugee community of thousands founded the first Vietnamese Buddhist temple in Phoenix. There was even a Buddhist scout troop to go with the temple, complete with uniforms and weekly meetings. Every Saturday thereafter, we children learned the way to nirvana and how to tie knots, and every Sunday, we recited Bible verses and contemplated hell.

My parents stressed that good deeds earn blessings, fulfillment, and wisdom not only for this life but also for the next life, and the next, and the next. That's why there are multiple Buddhas, male and female: They're humans who ascended to Buddhahood through many lives. You can imagine what bad deeds and bad lives reap. I was asked how I'd like to come back as an animal or a plant. And those weren't the worst options.

We can't pick the life we're born into, and so many things remain out of our control. The Middle English word for fortune, chance, luck, or lot was "hap" or "happe." From it comes haphazard, hapless, happenstance, perhaps. If you've experienced more good luck than bad, you're happy.

Whatever happens, at least how you react gives you a chance to determine your fate. No matter your family, ethnicity, economy, geography, or society, this is the only thing in your control: How you realize your dreams and rebuild after nightmares.

Ba Noi certainly had to constantly rebuild her life through the ever-rolling tides of wars, governments, and fortunes. She lived several lives in one. So did Grandma Mary.

Six

MARY EDNA SIMONS
(born March 19, 1923)

Arvada, Colorado
March 19, 1985

Dear Bob,

How's Carol Anne, and grandsons Bob and Keith?

The last of the babies have been picked up from our daycare center, and John has gone down for a nap. I'm tired, too, but I thought I'd take this chance to write you back. Your birthday card arrived today, right on schedule. Thank you for your wishes. Though now that I'm sixty-two, my wishes for myself are a lot simpler than when I was your age.

I have to tell you that after getting your card, looking after these little kids felt different. I kept seeing your face in those babies. At one point, giving one of the boys his bottle, it struck me that I was only twenty when I had you. Twenty! That's considered too young to have babies these days.

You wrote so much on the card, with so many questions about my life, and all those questions brought the past all back to me. It was difficult concentrating on the kiddie nursery here at our house in suburban Denver when my mind was filled with memories from Muscatine, Iowa.

I guess that's why I'm sitting here writing instead of taking a nap. I'm too restless. I'll try to answer your questions as best I can. Though knowing how you like to record things on computers, this will end up in a bound copy someday, so I'm feeling nervous about how I express myself. I'm uncertain how to begin. Should I be more formal than how I usually write to you?

I guess I'll just start.

My mother's mother, Mary Kendrick Berry, was a very refined, dignified lady from England. She came to the U.S. and somehow met and married John Peter Berry. What a mismatch. He was a mean, penny-pinching Pennsylvania Dutchman. Grandma Berry bore him four children. Then she lost her mind from living with him. Though it was never established that he was a wife beater, he definitely was a child abuser. He often beat his kids until blood ran down their backs. All but my mom. She was his favorite.

I can remember Grandma Berry sitting in the corner of the kitchen quietly humming, or sitting in her old, rickety rocker by her bed. She suffered terrible migraine headaches. Grandma didn't talk much, and never when Grandpa was home. When she had a migraine, she would have to be held down in bed by as many as six people. Her migraines would last two to three days. Once when I was small, she had a particularly bad night and somehow bolted from under the sheet and dove out the window. They caught her three blocks away. After several attacks like that, she was admitted to the state asylum.

I must have inherited her migraines, and when they struck me, Grandma sat and rocked me and let me listen to a beautifully engraved pocket watch she wore around her neck. She told me that when I was a big girl, I could have the watch.

Bob, I just read what I wrote. This is tiring. I'm all emotional. I'm stopping here. John's awake now anyway. I'm sure you'll have more questions after reading this.

— Mom

***

Arvada, Colorado
April 19, 1985

Son,

My father was James Earl Simons, born to Meyer and Alice Simons. Because Dad's mother died young of tuberculosis, at thirty-two, little is known of her. Even her children didn't know her very well.

Grandpa Simons told his kids that he was a riverboat captain on the original Delta Queen Excursion. The boat used to travel the Mississippi River between St. Louis and New Orleans. Near St. Louis, presumably on one of his trips, he met a Cherokee Indian girl. He fell in love with her. They married in St. Louis and lived on a houseboat on the Mississippi. They "shelled" from St. Louis to Minneapolis from the first thaw to the first freeze. Shelling was big business in those days. Muscatine, Iowa, was the "pearl button capital of the world."

Grandpa Simons made a lot of money, but much of his wealth was spent on medical bills and funerals. Dad told me about one time when he got typhoid fever, he had to be dropped off the riverboat in Minneapolis until the family could come back six weeks later. Grandma Simons became frailer. So did the children. They gave up the river life and moved into Muscatine.

Grandpa Simons was a kind man. He was serious except when I had a migraine headache. Then he'd come help Mom take care of me. I was his "Mulligan Stew" and "Molly Brown." It was at these times that he would tell me about Grandma, but I was only four or five.

Grandpa Simons had a beautiful trunk in one corner of the living room. The lid was like a dome, or rounded. It had alternate strips of leather and flowered brocade. Once you raised the lid, it had a removable shelf. I never saw the inside of the trunk, but I guess I just knew it was his private world. There were pictures of Grandma, but no one ever saw them. I could look at the trunk. I *could sit on it. But he wouldn't let me open it. On a few occasions, I saw him kneeling on the floor, trunk open, crying. Anytime he had it open and I'd try to peek inside, he'd take my hand and say, "Well, Mulligan, it's time we take a walk." I'd ask what was in there, and he'd just squeeze my hand and say, "Someday you will know. Some day." He would close the lid and a key on a long chain would come out of his pocket. He'd lock the trunk and place the key back.*

In later years, Grandpa had to move into a small shack, but the trunk went along. Grandpa died around 1939 at the age of eighty-seven. I was sixteen or so. While he was being buried, someone actually broke into his little shack and stole the contents of the trunk. We were all stunned and upset. The contents probably included the last of the information available about Grandpa Simons' family and the Cherokee Indian he loved and married. When I think of the double loss, I still get so mad.

— Mom

* * *

June 6, 1985

Bob,

I can't help getting distracted as I try to answer your questions. Once you let the past back in, you never know what gets through. I want you to know that it's flattering, your interest. I'll leave it to you to edit this down somehow. I know I'm rambling about stuff nobody else cares about except me. And maybe the grandkids, though your boys are already teenagers. If I'm lucky, future great-grandkids will be able to see that I was once a kid just like them. I know that a lot of things change with time, but there are just some things about childhood that never change, don't you think? Wanting toys, getting in trouble with your parents ...

To get back to it, there was only a five-year difference between me and Earl "Junior," but we were never close. Though I'm sure being an only child for so long had spoiled me, my father's doting over his son didn't help. In later years, Junior caused much heartache and many spankings for the rest of us because he could do no wrong. Daddy's boy turned out to be a monster, a real Dennis the Menace!

I was five when we moved north to Davenport, then there was Junior and one on the way, Alice. Our first house there, God forbid, was right off the railroad tracks. The Rock Island Line — now Amtrak. The first night we slept there, I thought I'd go crazy. It seemed like the trains were going to run right over us. We hated the place!

Pregnancies became a way of life with Mom from then on. She had seven: Five lived and two died. Nonetheless, pregnancies were never discussed. I never knew my mom was going to have a baby. I was always told that she was going to be sick. On a cold winter evening, I was about eight and had gone to a girlfriend's to play paper dolls. When I got back to my house, it was dark. Daddy wasn't home yet and I couldn't find Mom. Finally, I looked in the bedroom and there she was, asleep but moaning. I raced next door. They ordered me to stay there and ran over to my mom. Daddy came home and saw all the commotion. Mom went to the hospital a short time later in the neighbors' car. That was her first hospital delivery. The next morning, I was told that she had another brother for me, Elmer Leroy "Bud."

Sorry Bob, but my hand is suddenly cramping up. I'll write more next time.

***

June 30, 1985

Dear son Bob,

My mom had an Aunt Ruth and Uncle Larry who lived two blocks away in a nice apartment. He and Dad made homebrew beer during Prohibition days. That was illegal, so they would plant me on the front porch to watch out for any cops who might walk along. Boy, did I worry! After ten days, when the beer had fermented and was ready to bottle and cap, they made the beer in a 20-gallon crock and then ran a hose from inside the crock to each bottle. You would have to siphon the beer through the hose and naturally, you'd get a mouthful; forty-eight bottles made for a couple of silly guys. Mom and Aunt Ruth would make popcorn balls while Dad and Uncle Larry bottled the beer.

Each would end up with a big headache. My daddy couldn't hold his beer at all and would fall asleep in the corner.

Uncle Larry worked as an engineer at the Rock Island Arsenal, so we thought they were rich. Times were getting bad. Daddy's work was dropping off to two or three days a week. Uncle Larry would want to give Daddy money to buy groceries or pay his insurance — 25 cents a week — but Dad would refuse. The Great Depression worsened, Dad's health began to fail, and we moved from those railroad tracks to Myrtle Street. Our house might have been a shabby little one, but Mom always had shiny windows and starched curtains.

Meals got skimpier; many times, we didn't know where the next loaf of bread was coming from. One day, Uncle Larry and Dad were walking, and my dad got more and more tired and depressed, so he and Uncle Larry sat down on the curb. Dad cried because his insurance policy was lapsing that week. He needed 50 cents. All of a sudden, he looked down at the water running along the curb and there was a 50-cent piece! It was there on that curb that my dad got down on his knees and prayed. And we started going to the Lutheran Church every Sunday. I always suspected that Uncle Larry planted the 50 cents. Several times, Dad would ask his boss for a raise and more hours. I remember him coming home in tears because he was only able to get a 2-cent-an-hour raise and no more days.

School became hard for me. Mainly because I had so many migraine headaches and they'd sometimes last a day or two. I couldn't stand the pain and had to ride them out in a dark room. I averaged one or two a week. I stayed back — failed second grade.

I can feel one coming on right now just writing these words. Bob, I'm sorry, but I have to stop.

***

Arvada, Colorado

Dear Bob Lee Elston Sr.,

Happy birthday, forty-three-year-old! John and I hope this letter gets to you right on July 29. What do Carol Anne and the boys have in store for you? I'm so glad you agreed that my story will be of interest to future great-

grandkids. That's a great suggestion you have for me to explore what was fun in my childhood. For their benefit ...

In Davenport, Iowa, I had a girlfriend named Michaela whose mother went to work every day. They lived just down the street. After school, I'd go with Michaela to her apartment and stay until her mom came home at 5 p.m. We imagined that we were grown girls living together and dress up in her mom's clothes and play house, even though we were only six or seven. When her mom returned from a hot day working in the laundry, she'd give me a hug and a cookie and send me home.

Another baby — Anna Elizabeth — was on the way, so my family moved to a big home on the hill, a well-kept German neighborhood. I changed schools, and Michaela and I saw each other only at church. Our new house was right next door to Michaela's cousin, Irene. Their families didn't associate, though, and Mom explained to me that it was because Michaela's dad had run off and left her mom when she was a baby. Irene wouldn't even speak to her cousin Michaela. Irene and I soon got to be friends, but she was very spoiled and moody. She had a playhouse in the backyard that I thought was a mansion. Though we played in it all day long in the summer, it wasn't like playing house in Michaela's apartment. Michaela and I actually tried to clean, dust, and make food for her mom. That was so much better than pretending in a fake mansion.

Work picked up, but Dad began to have bouts of rheumatism. It grew harder and harder for him to get out of bed and get ready for work.

One Christmas, when I was about eight, I walked downtown and was shopping around. At the big and fancy M.L. Parker department store, a clerk walked up to me and said, "Oh, you came back for your purse," and shoved a small, black patent leather purse into my hand. She walked away. The toy section was full. I opened the purse and saw a bunch of change. Temptation got hold of me, and I left. Once outside, I discovered 63 cents in the purse. On West 3rd Street downtown was a Prinz fruit and vegetable market, and as I walked past, I saw fruit baskets of all sizes wrapped in beautiful red and green cellophane paper. I went in to ask how much one of those baskets cost, and Mrs. Prinz said about $2 to $5. I was disappointed. I wanted in the worst way to take one home to my daddy. I guess my disappointed face and the Christmas season overpowered her because she and her husband got their heads together and fixed my dad a small but beautiful basket for 50 cents. I ran the two-and-a-half miles home. My dad was so overwhelmed that he cried.

This was how rough it was for him: Two men would come in in the morning, carry Dad out to the car, take him to work, then carry him up the steps and set him on his bench, and that's where he'd stay until he had to go to the toilet or lunch. Then they would carry him back to the car and into the house. This went on for six months. Then a man across the street came over to talk to my dad about letting his chiropractor work on him. The neighbor had been like Dad until his doctor cured him. Twenty-five cents a treatment; three treatments a week. Dad said he couldn't afford it. Later that night, the doctor came over to beg dad to let him try: "I cure, you pay. I don't, you don't." He gave the first treatment free and Dad began to feel better, so then my parents really cut corners to come up with the money. After the treatments, Dad was well and walking under his own power.

We had lots of fun that summer: picnics, rides, and occasional ice cream cones. Dad and a neighbor planted a garden, and we had lots of vegetables. Work improved. He got a 5-cent-an-hour raise and was able to buy an old car. A Model B Ford, I think. Our house even had a toilet stool in the basement that flushed! No more outside trots in that twenty-degrees-below weather. We had a three-burner kerosene stove instead of a coal one. Real uptown. Even a water faucet, though still cold water. It was a big house, big enough for my sister Alice (she was four then) and me to have a playroom upstairs. All for $25 a month. I started junior high that fall.

***

Arvada, Colorado
September 9, 1985

Dear Bob,

I'm really sorry that it's been a while since I wrote. I don't know where August went. Arthritis has just taken over my life. I wake up with it and go to bed with it. It's like a new husband. I didn't expect old age to start this early, but then I keep forgetting I'm in my sixties. That is until a migraine hits, or arthritis, or when they both come together. I'm so tired of my body. At least the migraine is almost like an old friend. This arthritis, I'm not liking him one bit. Enough about old age.

Major holidays were always big events whether we had money or not. In the early years, presents were plentiful, but during the leaner years and as more kids arrived, it took skimping and scraping to come up with one present each.

I remember when the Shirley Temple dolls came out, I wanted one so badly. That was the only thing I wanted in the whole wide world. One night I heard Mom and Dad talking, and Mom had seen a replica for a couple of dollars. Junior wanted a wagon, Bud a trike, so my parents went to Holbrook Furniture Company, opened up a charge account, and got them. The payments were something like $2 a month, and Dad had a hard time meeting them.

I remember another hard Christmas when my gifts were slips and underpants made of bleached Pillsbury 25-pound flour sacks. Mom embroidered over the row of XXX's printed on them. Pretty lace was sewn on the pants and slips if she could scare up some.

Uncle Larry and Aunt Ruth were childless, so they spent Christmas Eve with us. First, we'd go to church, then we'd come home and Dad and Uncle Larry would have some of their homebrew. When I was six, my dad started setting an alarm clock for 6 a.m. for us to get up. Finally, one Christmas Eve, I rebelled and said that when I grew up and had kids, I would never make them wait until morning for Santa to come. And, Bob, I never did with you and your brother and sister.

About 10 o'clock Christmas morning, Grandpa Berry and Clara (his second wife) would drive up and come in with their 25-cent present for each. Mom's father had ceased (at Clara's demand) to shower us with gifts. No one showed much love for Clara, including Mom, for reasons I'll explain another time.

Chicken was the fare for the day. Thanksgiving and Easter were the same. Chicken. It was unheard of to have chicken outside special occasions. Mom would scrape together the money to buy one big chicken and, somehow, that chicken fed six to eight people. One of my pet peeves at big family dinners was that the kids must wait until all the adults had eaten before we could eat, and Grandpa Berry and Clara ate like horses, so wings and the part that went over *the fence last were waiting for us kids. I suspect that a lot of the time, Mom didn't eat much so that we could have something to eat.*

Although Grandpa Berry had a whole backyard garden, never once did he offer us a tomato from his vines. He had bought a 10-acre farm and raised cows, chickens, and pigs. He and Clara would brag about all the vegetables they gave to the neighbors. All the eggs, pork, and beef. Even when we visited them, not one time did they ever send us home with a speck of food. Not even when we were destitute. Once, Grandpa caught Junior, Alice, and me in the grape arbor, and did we get the devil! Wow! You would have thought we stole money. My hatred began to build for Grandpa Berry.

***

September 11, 1985

Bob,

Did my last letter shock you? Was I too harsh? I struggle with myself and this anger I still feel about my bitter childhood. I often ask myself what Jesus would have done in my place.

You're laughing at me, I know. Which brings me to this question for you for a change: At what point did you become an atheist? Was it something your father and I did? Was it our divorce (even though you were in your thirties already), or your having to fight in the Vietnam War?

What about my grandsons? Is Carol Anne religious?

I worry about your souls. There, I've said it and I'll say no more.

***

Arvada, Colorado
September 27, 1985

Bob, please tell Carol Anne happy birthday from us. Did she get our card? Back to your questions.

After we moved to Davenport in 1928, I didn't see Grandma Berry again. Five summers later, when I was ten, she died of a stroke at sixty. I don't think Mom ever believed that story, and I don't know why. Anytime we went to

Grandpa's after that, it didn't seem the same. A year later, Grandpa Berry brought a short, fat lady to our house and announced that she was his new wife, Clara. He told me I had to call her grandma, and I said that I wouldn't, that she was nothing like my real grandma. My mother sent me to my room without dinner. While my mom and dad were giving me a lesson in respect, they overheard Clara tell Grandpa to get a "snot-nosed" baby away from her, that she had no use for kids or she would have had some of her own. Mom and Dad were appalled and told me they were sorry they punished me, and that I didn't have to ever call her Grandma. The "snot-nosed" kid Clara was talking about was my brother Bud.

The first time we were invited to Grandpa Berry's house after Grandma died, Mom and her sisters all came. To their shock, they found the house totally remodeled and newly furnished. Every piece. Even an inside bathroom. They were also told after the initial tour that no one — but no one — would be allowed in "Clara's parlor." That was hard for me because I could still see Grandma lying in her casket between the two front windows and me sitting quietly on a stool nearby, waiting for Jesus to reach down with that long arm to take her to Heaven to live with him. Now, this fatty was telling me I could never go in that room again. I wanted to go home and never come back to that house.

Stories could go on, but what's the use? I'll save the final blow for later.

***

Arvada, Colorado
September 29, 1985

Son,

Whatever the doctor prescribed worked. I'm getting relief from both the migraine and arthritis.

Yes, Bob, I know, I hear you about John and me not getting enough exercise, and I know we should get out of the house more. I hear it from your dad, too, whenever he stops in here on his walks around the neighborhood.

Where was I? Oh, a highlight of my childhood was going down to the levee to watch the big excursion boats, three stories high, come in to dock several times a summer. People parked on the levee and sat in their cars to listen to a man way up on top play a steam-powered calliope. Do you know what that is? It had a keyboard, like a piano. When he finished a song, everybody would honk their horns for him to play again. The playing and the honking went on until nine, when passengers were all aboard and ready for a night of dancing to a band. The boat would move away from the levee, drift down the river about twelve to fifteen miles, and return by midnight.

I remember the names of the boats — The Capital and The Delta Queen II. The Capital was the newest and so beautiful. I always dreamed that someday, I would ride on that beautiful boat. I finally did when I was dating your dad. I asked him to take me on it. In those days, that was considered forward for a girl to ask for a date. Come to think of it, are girls asking your boys out?

— Mom

* * *

October 1, 1985

Dear Bob,

My sister Alice and I played a lot together. Junior started fights with other kids and ran like a coward, and little sister Alice mopped up the mess. She'd start taking on the bigger kid and holler, "Run, Juny run." Junior ran and hid till the dust settled.

One of the men who was carrying Dad back and forth to work lost his little daughter to pneumonia, and he and his wife got rid of all the daughter's clothes right after the funeral. Coats, shoes, and everything else of their daughter's, they brought over to Alice. We can't be sure but a week later, Alice had a bad cold; two weeks later she was dead. God, what a blow! I remember the ambulance coming to take her to the hospital. When the man carried her out, I begged him to bring my sister back because she was all I had. She never came home. That was November 1934.

* * *

Arvada, Colorado
October 8, 1985

Bob,

I'm sorry I cut off so abruptly last time. I can't predict when some memory will hit me harder than others. I guess I hadn't thought about Alice for so long that writing about her ... I felt guilty. Does that make sense?

I'm afraid we've come to the part that is the worst for me. I've been so dreading going back to all this, remembering all of it again. I keep telling myself that once I get through this part, I'll find happiness. Of course, you know better, Bob; I can't lie to you. Then I tell myself that my life is great now, with my new husband and my little daycare babies. But it's so far into the future! And though I know how happy I am now, I still get scared thinking about how many horrible years I went through to get here.

Enough procrastination. Hope arthritis stays away so I can hold this pen steady.

In May 1935, my mother nearly died in a botched home delivery. As the doctor was removing the baby, he dropped her, and the baby hit her head on the end of the table and died.

Mom took a long time recovering from that one. I remember a young nurse who was brought in to live with us and do private-duty nursing. On the fourth day, she decided Mom wasn't getting any better and had her moved to the hospital. When I came home from school, an aunt told me my mom might go to Heaven, with baby Helen, who never had a day on earth. This was unreal. The churches in the neighborhood had prayer vigils, and strangers brought food and money.

Mom recovered, but then Dad's health worsened, and then the little old landlady came to tell us she had sold our house.

We moved into a flat over a grocery store. Mom and Dad knew the owners from Muscatine, and they knew and hated Grandpa Berry, so they helped us whenever they could. On Saturday evenings, when they closed the store, they left fresh produce and fruits that wouldn't keep over the weekend at the bottom of our stairs. I had only a couple of blocks to walk to junior high. I had two miles to walk to church when my father couldn't drive. Dad's condition wors-

ened over the next few years, to a point that he was taken to the University of Iowa Hospital. They did one operation and found the start of cancer. I was fifteen.

**

October 22, 1985

Bob,

In the meantime, I had gotten a summer job at Mercy Hospital. I had to live right there in the building, just through the swinging doors from the delivery room. There was no such thing as working eight hours a day, forty hours a week. I had one day off every two weeks and one weekend a month. I made $15 a month plus my meals. I gave half the money to my family.

When I worked at the hospital, I started at 7 a.m., maybe got lunch and then dinner about 5 p.m. I had to be back on the floor by 5:30 to either carry trays or give bedpans to mothers, etc., or I would work the elevator or the switchboard until 9 p.m. If I was lucky, I'd get to bed by 9:30 and maybe, just maybe, get a full night's sleep. If there were women in the labor department waiting to have babies, I had to sit with them and clean up the delivery room after the births. I can remember having as many as five in the labor rooms at once. And sleep or no sleep, I was back on the floor to pass out breakfast trays, pick them up, help with the baths, and on and on and on. But I loved it and wanted to be a nurse.

That winter was our hardest. Dad was bedridden; food was scarce. My clothes were worn out hand-me-downs. I'd come home and ask whether anyone had brought any clothes that day. More often than not, no. We had a coal stove in the dining room, but we ran out of coal and the grocers downstairs let us use theirs. I think they were the ones who called welfare.

Those people brought in food, clothes, and coal the next day. Mom was expecting number seven in March. Christmas was one of our best in years because the welfare lady, Miss Lillian O'Brien, took a personal liking to our family. She saw to it that I had new clothes, that the kids had new toys, and that there was plenty to eat. The Salvation Army brought a big box on Christmas Eve.

Even the church brought baskets at Thanksgiving and Christmas. I was almost sixteen and had my first taste of ham! I had never had turkey.

Months dragged on that winter, and Miss O'Brien made Mom go to a fancy specialist to deliver the baby — Barbara Jean. Barb lay in a crib next to Dad's bed. It was a shock to the doctors that as sick as he was, he could still get my mother pregnant.

Dad had to go back to the University of Iowa Hospital during Memorial Day weekend 1939. Relatives moved in to take care of us kids, and Miss O'Brien found Mom a room where she could be near Dad and earn her meals working in the hospital cafeteria. Then our one neighbor who had a phone got a call to round up as many blood donors as they could and come right away. We were able to get six donors and left by midnight. I wasn't the healthiest, but they took a pint of my blood, too. I was so weak, I had to be carried to the car. Iowa City was about 50 miles from Davenport, and I kept passing out. That Saturday morning, a pastor brought Mom home. Our father had died.

Grandpa and Clara came up. Two men from the church council came immediately. They helped make all the funeral arrangements. Because it was Saturday afternoon, the insurance office could not be reached, so when Mom had to pay $40 for the down payment on the cemetery plot and the casket, she didn't have it. I can still see her look up at her father, and Grandpa Berry begrudgingly said, "Well, I guess I can loan you the $40 until the insurance comes Monday." The church councilmen said, "You keep your money; we'll underwrite every dime your daughter needs, and if we never get it back that's OK, too."

My grandfather always carried large sums of money in Clara's purse. Often as not, close to a thousand dollars. So, do you wonder why I hated my grandfather?

**

November 1

Bob, as soon as I mailed off the last letter, I was so relieved and yet so upset that I doubted I'd be picking up my life again anytime soon. But here I am. I can't stop thinking about it, so what's the use of trying to avoid writing about it?

Mom received a widow's pension. A year after Dad died in the spring of 1939, Miss O'Brien offered Mom — who started working at thirteen but stopped when she got married — a job at the welfare society's daycare center. She could even bring Barb, so Mom went back to work. She worked there until Barb was ready for first grade, then Miss O'Brien got Mom a job at the elementary school as a custodian. It was two blocks from home and the pay was better. She was totally independent.

She kept working for decades, right up to her devastating heart attack in 1962. Mom was fifty-seven years old. She was hospitalized for nine weeks, but she continued having pains and shortness of breath for a decade and a half until she died.

Actually, Bob, I don't feel well. I think I'll go lie down.

***

November 14, 1985

Hey there!

Happy birthday to grandson Bob. Did he like our card? I hope it came today. But it's so hard to pick out a card that a seventeen-year-old boy would like. I guess he's not really a boy anymore. But then I still think of you as a boy sometimes. It's a hard habit for a mother to break.

I really appreciated your phone call and your concern about me after receiving my last letter. Like you said, I know I can take this as slow as I want. Still, getting a telephone call from you and actually hearing your voice helped me a lot. I'm all right now. I can go on.

***

November 16, 1985

Dear Bob,

I can't stop thinking about my mother. Who am I trying to kid? I loved her. But she was hard to get along with, and if she asked me to do something for her, I'd better not say no. Even when I had my own family. She was part of the reason we left Iowa. Your father got fed up with her demands and issued me an ultimatum — "The kids and I are moving to Colorado. You can come or you can stay" — with no argument from me. I was more than ready to leave, too.

It also seemed that every time Mom came to Denver, there would be a quarrel before she left. Oh, we had fun; she loved her grandchildren. She loved you best, Bob, and doted on you. But to sum it all up, if my mom had her way, none of her kids would have ever married. We would have lived with her and supported her and catered to her every demand. My sister Barb's husband gave her the same choice: "Your mother or me." They moved to St. Louis.

When I announced that Hal and I were going to get married on September 14, 1942, Mom made my life miserable. Right up until my wedding day, she maintained that she would not come. It wasn't until I started down the aisle that I saw her sitting there in a new navy silk dress she had taken time to make! There were no reasons for her actions. But to her, I did not have to get married. She was losing her breadwinner.

How's that for something to think about as Thanksgiving approaches?

***

Arvada, Colorado
November 30, 1985

Hi Bob,

How is grandson Keith spending his special day? What's he going to do with the birthday money I sent? I wouldn't even know what to get a modern fifteen-year-old boy. On TV, teenagers seem so much more sophisticated than I and my friends were at this age. Aren't you scared?

How was turkey day for you guys? We spent it at John's daughter's house, and I tried not to think about the past too much. But I did think about my last letter and realized I now have grandchildren who will get married soon. Not as soon as your dad and I married, I'm sure, but still, you better start preparing yourself.

***

Arvada, Colorado
January 6, 1986

Happy New Year, Bob! Thanks for the Christmas sweater and all the photos of Bob Jr. and Keith. We spent the holidays mostly at John's daughter's house. Lots of ham, which I know you disapprove of. But I've been in love with it since my first taste in my teens.

As usual, John and I spent New Year's Eve dancing at the club with your dad and Vi. They're like Fred and Ginger to our Laurel and Hardy.

I agree with your last letter that I should give more details about what it was like being a teenager. But it's so surreal going back to those years and being the same age as Bob and Keith are now. It's like my personal time machine. It makes me happy and sad. I take that back. Your sons have their whole lives ahead of them, and I see nothing but good things ahead. Their lives have been so much happier than mine was, so I'm confident in their future. I look forward to meeting whoever will be their wives. If I'm lucky and they don't wait too long to get married, I'll even get to meet their kids! I know, I'm getting ahead of myself. ...

By the fall after Dad died, we had left the church I was raised in. Dear friends of Mom's, Floyd and Naomi, took me to their church, St. Paul's Lutheran. One of the first Sundays there, a handsome young man came up to our friends and asked for an introduction. His name was Dick Nesseler. All the way home, my heart pounded as Floyd and Naomi told me what a wonderful young man he was. Dick had asked me if I would go out with him that evening, and I said I'd ask my mother. I did. And she asked Floyd and Naomi about him. Dick was twenty-two; I was sixteen. "Too old," Mom said. He had just graduated from Augustine College — "too old." That was Mom's answer to everything they said about him. Weeks went on, but I could not sway Mom. Dick and I continued to see each other at church; he sang in the choir and had a beautiful voice. But the bullheaded Dutch wouldn't budge.

In eleventh grade, I met a kid in one of my classes and he liked me. Jack was a year older and had a nice new car. Jack was a smart aleck, spoiled because he was a "change of life" baby and his brother and sister were much older. He threw temper tantrums in front of his father that used to leave me speechless, but he was good to me. However, he didn't like movies or dancing, so most of our dates consisted of spending the evening with friends riding around and going to eat before I had to be back by 9:30. I still longed to go out with Dick but was taught to "Honor thy Father and Mother." Though I was tempted, I never sneaked out or defied my mother. Dick just continued to be patient.

The following June, Jack graduated and gave me a diamond. It was small, but it was still something! My mother was heartsick. Jack and I continued to break up and make up. Dick went off to naval school and told Floyd and Naomi that when he graduated, I'd be eighteen and my own boss.

I had to give up school in the last half of my senior year, two credits short. Money ran out and my mom needed her half of my $15-a-month salary, so I was still working and living at the hospital.

In March 1942, after breaking up with Jack, I met a dashing, handsome young man at the roller rink. He asked me if he could drive me home that night. I said I didn't go out with strangers, so he said, "OK, my name is Hal." Hal took me home to the hospital.

That September — the Sunday before I married your dad — Dick Nesseler was home on leave. I was nineteen, and he felt this was his last chance. Before the church service, the pastor told him I was getting married. Dick congratulated me. "Do you love him?" I said, "Yes," and Dick said, "Well, I guess that's it then. I'll always love you," and walked away. I've never forgotten the look on his face.

***

February 2, 1986

Yes, Bob, sometimes I'd wonder what if... After your father and I divorced, my mother asked that question more than I did. But God just had other designs for me.

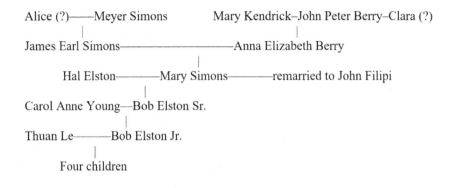

Alice (?)———Meyer Simons   Mary Kendrick–John Peter Berry–Clara (?)

James Earl Simons———————————Anna Elizabeth Berry

Hal Elston————Mary Simons————remarried to John Filipi

Carol Anne Young—Bob Elston Sr.

Thuan Le———Bob Elston Jr.

Four children

* * *

Arvada, Colorado
February 4, the Year of Our Lord 2003

Dear Bob,

I've just finished reading your edited version of my life story. I'm sorry it took me so long since you gave it to me as a Christmas present. I'm so slow these days. Everything takes so much more time than it used to. I don't know whether it's because I'm so weak now. Sometimes, I listen to myself talk and don't even recognize that it's me. And it's more than the fact that my voice has lowered an octave or two. I talk slower now; I sound like a turtle. The time it takes to form a sentence and then to say the sentence, I don't know what happens. Lucky you this is a letter.

I might show my life story to one person here at the nursing home. No, not my roommate. And don't worry, I don't have any old — and I mean old — boyfriend in this place.

As for grandson Bob's news about his posting to Indonesia (I hope I copied that correctly from your letter) and how you're all moving there together with MY great-grandkids, I hope you're joking. Really, you're not serious, are you? I'm the first to say I'm easily confused these days, but isn't Bali in Indonesia the same Bali where that terrorist bomb exploded and killed all those people at the night club? I know I'm pretty clueless about the world outside America, let alone outside the Denver area, but I'm sorry to say that I don't understand this at all.

On the other hand, your announcement that you're bringing everyone here to visit me before you move so far away is really good news. Let me know when so I can prepare the staff and all my friends here. I'll be the envy of the place.

To answer your final questions: You were named Bob after your dad's younger brother. Hal was very close to him in the early years, but as your Uncle Bob became a lawyer and got into politics, he outgrew his family. Especially after he became a Washington state Superior Court judge.

Your dad was pleased when you continued the name with Bob Jr., though Carol Anne told me once that part of the reason was you were shipping to Vietnam and you two weren't a hundred percent certain you'd be coming back, so you wanted your son to have your name. Thank the Lord that not only did you come back but that you came back whole. Except for malaria, and the tank explosion that got you the Purple Heart, you didn't suffer anything else, physically or mentally. You're like your dad that way, fit in body and strong in mind. No postwar syndrome for you.

***

She paused and looked up. Outside in the dark, one of those massive, noisy Colorado snowstorms was throwing its weight around. But her mind barely acknowledged it.

Mary looked down at what she just wrote. A vision of Bob in his crew cut and Army uniform rose in her mind, then melted into an image of a chubby baby boy. Where did 1943 go? She could still hear someone excitedly yelling, "It's a boy! Mary, your baby is a boy." But for the life of her, she can't remember whether it was Hal or a nurse. What she *did* remember was the plump, white blob someone placed in her arms.

When it came to my children, Mary thought, I truly learned the uselessness of being human. How can I explain it, my dear Lord? That we at our most basic level are just animals trying to protect our young. Only You elevate our existence.

My baby, my firstborn, we almost did lose him. Several times.

Vietnam, yes, but that was a war. He already was a man, married, and with his own child on the way. But when Bob was four months old, the doctor gave him only one month to live. He was projectile vomiting and couldn't keep down the milk formula. He couldn't keep down any liquid.

Mary closed her eyes.

I was desperate. Do you remember, my Lord? He had come from me and, even with death at the door, his cheeks were filled with rosy babyhood and a whole life ahead of him. I fed him mashed potatoes and whatever non-liquid food substance I could think of. That hateful doctor, he was doubtful. But what did I have to lose except everything? And You saw it: I won. Two weeks later, the doctor was amazed and said my son would live. Doctors!

Then came ninth grade. Spring 1958. Bob missed an entire semester because of a sudden bone disease, osteomyelitis. He was very active, athletic. What sport *didn't* he play? Lord, we thought it was just the usual growing pain. But he had a fever that wouldn't go away. And then the doctors diagnosed my boy with ... this thing that I wish I didn't know how to spell so well. He was confined to his bed for several months. Again, they said my firstborn was near death. Hal was so worried about our boy's mental faculties, he went into the hospital to play chess with Bob all the time. But again, my boy outlived the doctors and their expectations. Again, Lord, my son outlived my fear of losing him. Not only him but also his brother and sister. Can a mother ask for more, to die before her children?

***

"Has anyone here been to a Vietnamese wedding?" Grandson Bob's wife asked us nursing home residents. It's dark, except for the light coming from the soft screen pulled down in front.

I'd be surprised if anyone here had been to a non-American wedding. There weren't that many Orientals living in the area. If you lived in Denver or Colorado Springs, maybe, but not Arvada. Look at all of us, old Americans in our bathrobes and wheelchairs. White hair, white, papery skin. Mostly alert, I guess, grateful for this change of pace. We liked our routines here, except when it was boring.

It was a treat to have my granddaughter-in-law show us a video of when she and Bob Jr. got married in Southern California in 1995. I'm glad Thuan didn't mind when our activities director asked her. How comfortable she looked with the microphone up there in the front of the room, her voice not shaky at all, chatting as if it were a conversation just between her and me. How did she do that?

"A Vietnamese wedding usually has four parts: a ceremony in front of the ancestral altar at the bride's house, then a religious ceremony at a temple or church or whatever, another ancestral altar ceremony at the groom's house this time, and finally a dinner-dance reception. But Bob and I didn't have the religious part, and because the Elstons don't worship ancestors, we didn't have a ceremony at his house, either. Which is lucky for all of you today because you only have to sit through a two-part wedding. The American way." Thuan laughed, which I guess put my housemates at ease because I heard them chuckle around the room.

"Now, what you are seeing here is the groom's side arriving and lining up in front of the house. The groomsmen — aren't they handsome in their black tuxes — are carrying trays either wrapped in red or covered with red cloths. The red is for good luck, and the trays are meant to be bearing gifts for the bride's family — tea, sticky rice, roasted meats, cognac. Can everyone hear me all right? If I'm speaking too fast, please let me know."

I bet no one else here has an Oriental granddaughter-in-law. I bet my great-grandkids were the most gorgeous anyone here has ever seen. They were so adorable visiting me this week with their parents, skipping around yet so well-behaved. And the oldest was only five. Oh, there were some good kids at the daycare center John and I ran for a dozen years; we took care of some real charmers. But something about the Orientals, though. The children are usually so well-behaved.

Who'd ever have thought I'd have great-grandkids who are half Oriental! Until I married Hal in Davenport, I had never gone outside Iowa. For our honeymoon, he drove me to Memphis, Tennessee, but after that, it was right back to Iowa. We didn't move to Colorado until I was, what, in my thirties already? Now, out of my six grandchildren, Bob and Keith have traveled all over Asia. Isn't that funny? Most Americans go to Europe, but not them. I don't think it has anything to do with their father having been in the Vietnam War. My other son was with the Navy in Japan, and his kids aren't ... but what do I know. I haven't seen them in a long time.

I met Thuan in Irvine, California, where John and I had driven to visit son Bob and Carol Anne. Thuan was tiny. A little Oriental doll with that long, black hair. I didn't know what to expect. I wouldn't have been surprised if she had bowed or something, but I was so relieved when she didn't. And her English was so good. I said I was surprised her English was so good. Grandson Bob explained that Thuan had come to America when she was in grade school.

"And there's Grandma Mary in the wedding procession into my house," Thuan said as I appeared on the screen. "Isn't she pretty in her pink suit?"

Oh! There was John Filipi, still alive and walking beside me, years away from his heart just quitting on him. I didn't even think about this, that I would see my husband alive! It had been two years since he died, around 9/11, but it was like yesterday. I guess no one can be really dead anymore, really gone. With video, everyone can be ... immortal. It's impossible, I know, but I don't know how else to put it. Just think, if video had been invented earlier, I'd be able to make my parents live again on the tube anytime I wanted. My grandparents even! Well, maybe not Grandpa Berry the Scrooge.

Look at John's round face on top of that round body. I thought I was done with happiness after my divorce from Hal. But marrying John was like being reborn, twenty-two years of a new life. Imagine that — getting married first at nineteen then again at fifty-six. Two married names. What a soap opera. I never thought such drama would happen to me. I never asked for it.

"And many of you will recognize the couple walking behind Grandma Mary and her husband into the wedding. I understand that Grandpa Hal and Vi are regular visitors here."

"Where are they?"

"Shhh."

"Who's Hal and Vi?"

"Mary's first husband."

"Hush!"

"Who's Vi?"

"I think his new wife."

"Shhhh"

"What?"

Just listen to my housemates. But Vi, sitting in the back with Hal, her hair and face beautifully made up as usual, didn't seem to register the whispers. And Thuan kept talking as if she didn't hear the gossip, either.

"Here, these are some of my aunts and uncles lining the walkway to greet the groom's family. There are a whole lot more of them inside the house. My mother has ten sisters and four brothers."

It was standing room only inside that house. Just one person got to sit, Thuan's mother's mother. The matriarch. All her children were there, and it seemed all *their* children were there, too. Overrunning that house were old ones like us all the way down to babies being passed from hand to hand. I had never been surrounded by so many Orientals my whole life. We were definitely outnumbered, even with Carol Anne's sister and her sons, and friends from our side of the family.

"My father died several years before, so the oldest of my three brothers welcomed the groom's family. I was in my bedroom with my bridesmaids, waiting to be summoned out to the living room."

There they came, the four bridesmaids all in green traditional dresses, one of them Caucasian, then Thuan came out in pink. Not white! I know, I was confused, too. It was even more confusing when — look — a white-haired American escorted her out. A tall, lion of a man.

"This is Uncle Chauncey Collard giving me away. He's one of my aunts' husbands. He and my aunt were living in Sai Gon when the city fell to the communists and all my relatives were trying to escape. Through his job as an American pilot, he got papers for everyone in my mom's family to get on the planes to leave." Thuan paused and looked around the room. "Does anyone have any questions? Can everyone hear me OK?"

"You're doing fine," our activities director yelled out from the back of the room.

"Great. OK. So, on the screen right now, what my bridesmaids and I are wearing, and also most of the women and girls in our family, are traditional Vietnamese dresses, called ao dai, meaning literally long shirts. In Viet Nam, the color white is reserved for funerals, so white is not our traditional color for weddings. Wedding garments used to be red and gold, imitating the royal family. But now people pick whatever color they want. I don't know whether you can see the colors clearly in the video, but what I'm wearing is hand-painted pink silk. It has touches of light green in it and hints of gold, and a matching outer robe and a silk, halo-like turban for my head. I teased my bridesmaids that they were the leaves, and I was the flower. They still haven't forgiven me for it." Thuan laughed, and again I heard responding laughter from my housemates. Oh, I was so glad this was going well.

Just like her wedding had. No church, though. But I wasn't surprised. Bob and Carol Anne had never been religious, and Thuan's family is Buddhist, though her mother didn't even insist on a temple wedding. Bob Jr. and Thuan exchanged vows in front of her family altar, with photos of her dad and ancestors and smoke drifting from overpowering incense sticks.

Those red packages the groomsmen brought in went on the altar, along with a roasted piglet! Did all my fellow old Americans get a glimpse of this red-skinned thing on the video screen? It had crisply burned ears, a blackened squiggly tail, and a red carnation in its mouth. I should have been sick to my stomach, but my mouth started watering looking at the juicy, tender pork. I couldn't believe it.

"Bob and I wrote poems as our vows; mine in Vietnamese and Bob's in English."

It really was a touching ceremony, though it was so different, and I couldn't understand much of it. Still, I was witnessing the first of my grandchildren getting married. Bob crossed a threshold, and I felt he was taking the rest of the Elstons along with him.

"Instead of a limousine, we rented a convertible Model-T to take us to the dinner reception. Do some of you remember driving or riding in one of those?"

I had to say that man who drove the antique Ford went all out, dressing in newspaper-boy cap and knee-length britches, even tying cans and trinkets behind the old car. For the kids as well as us adults, it was like having a big toy. So many people wanted to take their pictures sitting in the Model-T before Thuan and Bob could get in it. But finally, off they went, circling the cul-de-sac and rolling toward the restaurant.

"This was a Chinese-Vietnamese seafood restaurant in Huntington Beach. We had more than two hundred guests, a real United Nations. My family alone was a hundred. Then there was the groom's side, all our journalism colleagues, and even old military friends of my father from South Vietnam! An older cousin of mine was the emcee for the night."

Uh-oh.

"Before my cousin brings the wedding party up on stage, he's going to introduce our parents and grandparents, in both Vietnamese and English."

Actually, it was kind of awkward. I don't think they were used to introducing grandparents who had been divorced. It wasn't what he said. It was the way he said it. Poor man, he struggled. It wasn't his fault we Americans aren't Orientals. I wonder how he said it in Vietmanese, or however you say it. Maybe it was best not to know. Here he went in English: "It is my honor to introduce to you the bride's maternal grandmother, Mrs. Nguyen Huu Tai."

Now, this was interesting. Thuan told me that's not her grandmother's name; it's the name of Thuan's grandfather, who died a long time ago. Women in Vietnam don't take their husbands' last name but, like us American wives, they're known as Mrs. whatever the husband's full name is. So because this widow had never remarried, she was still known as Mrs. ... whatever that man just said in the video.

I was sure Thuan had told me her grandmother's real name, but those foreign words all sound the same to me. The funny thing was I had admitted that to Thuan once, and she told me not to worry — to her grandmother, all American names sound the same, too. Wasn't that something?

"Please welcome the groom's paternal grandmother and her husband, Mary and John Filipi." John held my hand up the stage, with two hundred people applauding as if we had just won an Oscar. All that attention, just because we're the grandparents of one of the stars of the show.

"And the groom's paternal grandfather and his, hmm, girlfriend, Hal and Vi."

Poor Vi. Most of the people in this nursing home can't hear that well anyway, so maybe they weren't really listening to this. It wasn't Vi's fault. Hal had remarried once after he and I divorced, and that didn't work out, either. The second divorce proved so costly he vowed never to marry again. And Vi, after managing to escape from that brute of a husband who used to beat her, she also vowed never to remarry. She and Hal had been like an old married couple though, together since 1980-something.

I had to say I was happy for Hal when he found Vi. Vi was much more his speed anyway, dancing every weekend and traveling abroad. They even went to China together! I went to Mexico once and couldn't wait to get back to the good old USA.

I guessed we were an odd foursome. John and I used to live only a couple of blocks from Hal and Vi. Hal might not have worked out as a husband for me, but he was great as an ex. A true helpmate. Since John passed away ... what would I have done without Hal and Vi? They dropped in here at the nursing home at least once a week, taking me to the Old Country Buffet or a dance at the club.

Though our club had never been as noisy as Thuan and Bob's wedding; this video proved it. So many people trying to talk and laugh at once. John and I and Hal and Vi were seated with Thuan's grandmother. She couldn't speak English except "hello" and "thank you." We didn't know Vietmanese, I meant VietNamese, at all, so a lot of smiling was all we could manage.

It's a pity because I had all these questions for her. Fifteen children, how did she do it?

"Vietnamese brides these days also change for the cutting of the cake, so there I am in a white Western dress. The groom even changed into a white dinner jacket."

Look at my grandson! The spitting image of his father and grandfather. People seeing the three of them standing together always think they're seeing the same man at different stages in a long life. But I hope he hadn't inherited their pig-headedness, how they can't say they're sorry to save themselves, or their fear of mortality.

***

It's about time I had visitors in this nursing home. Other people get visitors all the time. But I understand: Bob and Carol Anne had been living all the way on the East Coast with Bob and Thuan and their kids — and Thuan's mom! It was the Oriental way, they told me. It must have been a big place, this house of theirs outside Washington, D.C. Hal and Vi visited them once and reported back that everything was ridiculously expensive.

Grandson Keith was the one who lived the farthest away, in Okinawa, Japan, working at a U.S. military base. It was where he met Mariko, which they explained to me is Mary in Japanese. Can you believe he was going to marry someone named like me except in another language? I couldn't wrap my head around that one. He brought Mariko to Colorado this week so we all can meet her. They wanted me to fly to Japan for the wedding. It was really sweet of them, but ...

Everyone was so far away nowadays. They went abroad as if they were just going to the corner store. Grandson Bob used to be a reporter, but his new job with the government was sending his family to Indonesia — not only him, his wife, and their kids, but son Bob, Carol Anne, and Thuan's mother were going along, too! They said they'll be back in a couple of years. In this war-on-terrorism world though, will they be back at all? I didn't want to show my ignorance by showing my fear. What did I know? They didn't seem nervous at all. Just the opposite; they were all so excited about traveling and sightseeing and shopping. Carol Anne was looking forward to having a housekeeper and a driver. Grandson Bob went on and on about looking forward to living outside America again. What was wrong with America?

It was funny, though, how two brothers in one American family are both marrying Orientals, Bob a Vietnamese and Keith a Japanese. Keith even had belonged to a fraternity at USC; you'd think he'd have his pick of gorgeous blondes just like him.

I asked son Bob once whether he minded at all that none of his grandchildren would look white. He answered that he never even thought about it in those terms. He did say, though, that Thuan didn't think her father would have been happy about her marriage if he were alive. She was the oldest of five, and her father had been very traditional Vietmanese.

I meant VietNamese. I kept having to remind myself of President Bush the elder saying Vietnam, but it's a hard country with too many consonants. I had a sneaking suspicion that I got it wrong every time I tried to say it, but that they were all too nice to correct me.

And to think that I had wanted so badly to believe I had a quarter Native American blood in me from my father's mother. Years ago, Hal and I had a woman trace our genealogy, and I found out that Grandma Alice Simons was from the Fox tribe in the Davenport area. But the disappointing part was, I also found out I had only an eighth Indian blood. I forget why. I can't remember the details. But I still wish that I were more Native American.

I guess it didn't matter anyway because the bloodline was really getting mixed now.

***

I must confess I was nervous when Bob called to say the whole family was flying here for a week! What if they found out?

Larry and I had been discreet, but you never know. We cuddled only when my roommate was safely asleep, though I sometimes wondered whether she faked that snore. I just hoped she wasn't a blabbermouth.

And really, what of it? John wouldn't have approved, but he was no longer here, was he? I didn't like John very much by the end, anyway. He had turned mean. When he had to be hospitalized and I was sick enough that I needed care myself, they offered for me to stay in the same room with him. I said no, thanks. It was sad, but by then I was experienced. I knew what falling out of love felt like from when my marriage with Hal fell apart. I recognized the symptoms.

I didn't care that Larry was four decades younger than I was; I really didn't. He was the best nurse in the whole place, and he always appreciated the little things about me. It made it all worthwhile to get up in the morning, or from my afternoon nap, and prepared my face to meet him. I felt like a girl again when he was with me. It felt as if we were sneaking around in a college dorm, not a nursing home. What I imagined a college would be like anyway; it made up for my not ever having been.

Don't get me wrong. I wasn't feeling sorry for myself. I had worked hard for everything I had, and we were very comfortable by the end. Comfortable enough for me to buy my grandsons gold watches, with little diamonds in them, as college graduation presents. Comfortable enough that when I remembered what nothing I had when I was their age, I couldn't believe it.

It felt as if it were another life. Actually, it felt as if it were someone else's life; I had to remind myself that I lived it.

Even after marrying Hal, I had nothing. He gave me two boys, and then the military took him for World War II. At least he didn't get sent to the front. Because he had lost his left eye in a childhood accident and had a glass one, they only sent him to Florida to guard German prisoners. But his basic training salary was puny, and I was expected to pay for all our living expenses with it. It got to the point where I was going to be evicted from our rental, so I wrote our congressman, and he helped me get Hal an emergency discharge through the Red Cross. Hal got home to a mountain of bills. It took three years to pay all the debts, and the only vehicle we had was a coaster wagon with sides — $10 a week on it until it was paid for.

I didn't know how I made it through. If someone had told me I'd have to go through such bad times first to get to the good times, I'm not sure I would have been brave enough to wake up every day. But wake up I did. Each morning came and I'd just put one foot in front of the other. Two little helpless boys depended on me, and I just concentrated on their survival one day at a time until Hal returned.

***

"So what did everyone think?"

"It was interesting all right."

Look at Carol Anne, staring straight ahead as she answered

Thuan. I wondered whether she just didn't want to look at her daughter-in-law, or whether she was really trying to concentrate on driving. It reminded me of whenever Edith Bunker got the third degree from her daughter on television, about some social/cultural issue or other, and Edith avoided Gloria's eyes and just tried to get through the conversation and back to familiar ground.

All in the Family tried to deal with all sorts of issues. Sometimes it went too far, but it was still one of my favorite TV shows. I liked Edith. She was like a friend I got to see once a week.

I was glad Carol Anne concentrated on the road as she was driving, anyway. It rained before we got to the movie theater, and now it was so dark even the streetlights were barely cutting through this downpour. They were taking me back to the nursing home. Some ladies' night out. *The Hours* wouldn't have been my first choice for a movie outing, nor my last. It was dark and confusing, and depressing. What was so entertaining about that?

"Hmmm. Some of the American terms I never heard before. It was difficult for me to understand."

You weren't alone, Mariko. It was difficult for *me* to understand.

"It was too strange for me. All those women kissing each other! Yuck."

I knew I could count on Vi! I didn't want to say anything, but yuck was right.

"Yeah, what was that all about? They're not all lesbians, right?"

Thuan answered Carol Anne: "I don't think it has anything to do with being lesbian. Well, OK, except those characters played by Meryl Streep and Allison Janney, of course. Their kiss at the end was all about wanting love from each other, but the others were not."

Vi said, "Well, I should hope that Virginia Woolf wasn't kissing her sister because they were lesbians!"

"Oh no, she wanted what her sister possessed. That kiss and the one by Julianne Moore's character to her neighbor — played by what's her name, Toni Collette — were about wanting a personality trait that you don't have, wanting to suck it away from the person who has it into yourself."

Really?

Carol Anne said, "I almost didn't recognize Toni Collette. I've never seen her so sexy."

I didn't even know who Toni Collette was. But of course, Carol Anne kept up with all the popular culture. Whenever she and Bob visited and we watched TV together, I could always count on her to explain to me who's who.

I had never been a big fan of going to the movies, anyway. It was too expensive. But Thuan insisted on paying for all our tickets tonight. It was as if she had guessed ahead of time that *The Hours* would be too weird for the rest of us. And it was. I didn't understand any of it. It was a lot to take in.

What did Virginia Woolf have to kill herself over? She had a husband who loved her, who slaved away at that print shop so she could do what she wanted with her life — to write. Even in my worst of times, I never thought I had the right to kill myself. It's a sin against God, who made us. Now I'm glad I never tried to read anything by Virginia Woolf. And that other woman, that redhead from the 1950s, she was beautiful. She had absolutely beautiful clothes and a husband who came back from World War II who gave her a perfect house and a son. If I had her life, I'd never think of walking away like that. It was heartbreaking that she abandoned her son and her responsibilities. No wonder that boy turned out so messed up.

There was another thing bugging me. "Why ... why did that redhaired woman check into a hotel all by herself?"

"Grandma," Thuan answered, "she wanted to read. Well, it was more than reading. She just wanted to escape and be her own person."

"Her own what?"

"I think that she just felt like society told her she had to have a husband and must reproduce. Don't you think it was tragic in the end when she practically confessed that she had never wanted to be a mother in the first place? But she just ... decided that she had to be true to herself, that she couldn't pretend anymore. She just realized she was acting out some part society had assigned her, and she decided to leave the stage and really live for herself. You know?"

I don't remember any of this. "You saw all that?"

"Hmmm, really?" Mariko asked. "How do you know? Thuan, you saw this movie before?"

"I read the book. It's probably already translated into Japanese, Mariko. We can probably find it on Amazon."

If you asked me, it sounded like work. I never did like shows that made me do too much work to enjoy them. Now, *Gomer Pyle*, that was a good time. I wish I could have followed Jim Nabors when he left show business and moved to Hawaii. Of course, that was just a healthy daydream. I never would have abandoned my responsibilities or people who depended on me.

***

Her own person.

Can't sleep. That damn movie. Just listen to my roommate snoring. How is anyone supposed to sleep with all this? Did I ... Maybe the night nurse forgot to give me my pills after "the girls" dropped me off.

I could tell them a thing or two, my daughter-in-law and her two daughters-in-law. Vi could, too. But nobody asked us anymore. Once you were old, they just assumed things about you and didn't bother asking you anything anymore.

To hear Thuan speak about that movie tonight, you'd think she was a film reviewer, or a book critic, or something like that. But she wasn't. Where did she come off thinking she knew so much more than we did? Such conviction about what she knew. Where did she get the gall?

Sigh. Sorry, Lord, I shouldn't be so harsh on Thuan. I didn't know about Mariko, and Keith told me the Japanese are extremely polite people. But Thuan had been in America since she was a kid. If you closed your eyes and listened to her, Thuan was American. Modern, and whatever that went with it.

Thuan was nice and kind to me in her own way. But I understood — she wasn't really interested in me. I was just her husband's grandmother. I can't express myself very well. I even talked slowly, while she just rattled away a mile a minute. I didn't even know what to talk to her about. I had never finished high school. And here, English wasn't even her first language and she was some sort of editor at some big American newspaper.

She was just young, wrapped up in her here and now, and I can understand that, Lord. I remembered how selfish I was when I was younger.

Hal had always been the one with the more interesting stories to tell. The boys were always asking him for more, how he started with nothing but worked so hard to overcome his odds: the Army, owning a grocery store, getting a college degree later than he should have, his days as a traveling salesman with Dun & Bradstreet. Hal could even spin stories about his parents, a janitor and a homemaker who both are now part of the dust in Columbus, Nebraska. They were mythical somehow.

Meanwhile, I was just a wife and mother. I didn't have a business until I was already old: the daycare center with my second husband. For a while, back in the '80s, my oldest son wanted me to write down my life story, and I sent him letters about it. He had questions, and I tried to answer them as best I could. I did, Lord. I tried.

Some answers you had to keep for yourself, though. Some answers belonged to nobody else but you. You owed yourself that much.

I mean, Hal was a traveling salesman. He loved what he did. He investigated and wrote credit reports on businesses large and small. Hal was among the best of Dun & Bradstreet's hundreds of salesmen in the USA. In the early 1950s, he covered southern Iowa and western Illinois. Then he expanded to Colorado, southern Wyoming, and northern New Mexico. He didn't quit until 1969.

While my husband was out traveling and having such a fulfilling career, there were a lot of days and weeks of those two decades when I felt I was a single mother. More if you counted Hal's stint guarding German POWs in Florida.

Oh, Lord, don't get me wrong. I was fulfilled; really, I was. I wanted to be a mother. I wanted children. I loved children. After mine were grown, I took care of other people's children. I didn't need society forcing wifely and motherhood duties on me. I felt lucky I got the job! But Hal had adventures. Not that he didn't work hard. That wasn't true. But I worked hard, too, even if it was at home. Didn't I get any credit for that? I should have gotten a medal for bravery, a bonus for endurance.

Though I had to admit, Lord, once in a while, I didn't want the job at all. I'm not telling You anything You didn't already know. You were there. You saw lots of mornings when I woke up at my wits' end, having to remind myself that this was what I wanted, being a wife and mother. There were lots of times when I woke up not wanting to be me at all, but I still played me, and I forced myself to be me. It felt like that anyway.

I know, I know, Lord, that I wasn't the only one who experienced this. I'm sure it happened to Hal, and I know it happened to our children when they became parents, and to their children. From all the stories my family has shared I can see that it was timeless, this tug of war, this dreading what you wanted, what you desired.

It wasn't bound to any one generation. Love and duty crossed generations.

It must be universal, too, now that I think about it. I mean, Thuan's grandmother with those fifteen children ... what a ninny I was to feel sorry for myself when I raised only three! What that poor woman must have gone through; just think of *her* sacrifices. All the way across the world, did she also have days when she just wanted to escape, when she wished she were somebody else? How did she cope? Was her culture really that different from ours when it came to motherhood?

That was what she and I could have talked about when we sat next to each other at our grandchildren's wedding reception. Instead, we might as well have been deaf and dumb because of our language barrier.

I was dying to know whether she ever used the same trick I did: On the rough days, if you just continued to play your role as a mother, then life could continue, and you could get past it until you felt like yourself again. My Dear God, that was how I managed to stay at my post all those years. I didn't want to betray my husband and my young children. I didn't want to betray myself in Your eyes, oh Lord. I wanted to stay true to myself. I never left my post like that redheaded woman in that movie, when my family still needed me.

Which was why I just didn't understand what Thuan said tonight. What did she mean that the redhead was "just being true to herself"? I mean, I understood the pursuit of happiness, and I understood that happiness was a good thing. On the other hand, Lord, it wasn't as if a choice was an independent thing, born out of nowhere. Not so. Someone made that choice.

It was like what I heard in a cowboy movie the staff showed us this week in the main room. What was that thing Clint Eastwood said?

The dwarf asked the drifter something like, "What do we do when it's over?"

And the drifter answered, "Then you live with it."

When I heard those words, I looked around at all these old souls waiting to die with me in this nursing home, and I said, "Amen!"

***

"Hi, Mary! Look who's here," Hal exclaimed in a bright voice to his first wife. "Son Bob has made it back from Indonesia. He couldn't bring all our beautiful great-grandkids with him, but he brought the oldest one."

The sun was setting on a June evening in 2004. Hal gingerly picked up Mary's hand to try to get her to look at him, but she continued to stare out the window of her hospice room, where the medical staff had moved her after she suffered a stroke.

Bob, seeing his mother for the first time since the family visit more than a year ago, tried to hide his shock at how different she looked, gaunt and ... not there. He squeezed his grandson's hand, borrowing some strength to steady his voice before speaking. "Hi, Mom! Can you hear me? Everyone wanted to be here, of course, but Bob and Keith just couldn't get away from work. They all send their love, Mom. Mom? ... Dad, I thought your e-mail said she was more aware than this."

"Well, she's managed to smile and nod. I didn't write anything about her talking. Mary? Mary, look who Bob brought back to see you! It's Tigger. Your poor great-grandson was so jet-lagged, he slept until almost five this evening, but now he's up and he's here visiting with you."

"Actually, Dad, now that he's in first grade, he prefers to be called Rocket T."

"Oh, is that what you like to be called? Rocket T?"

"Ssss."

"What did he say? Little man, my ears aren't so good anymore, so I give you permission to yell at me. OK?"

"Dad, he said yes. Rocket, you'll have to speak up."

"Mary, it's Rocket T! Tell Great-Grandma how old you are now."

"I'm six and a half," the boy said, then froze where he stood as his great-grandmother's head slowly turned toward him.

Bob looked at his father in wonder, then he pulled the boy closer to the bed. "Mom, your oldest great-grandchild is a first-grader. Where we're living in Jakarta, Indonesia, the kids go to an international school that has students from sixty-five countries!"

Mary's eyes began to flicker on and off.

"Rocket, here. Squeeze her hand." Bob curled his grandson's fingers around his mother's. "Mom, can you feel your great-grandson's fingers? Concentrate on his fingers, Mom. Hey, Rocket T-Man, she likes hearing your voice. Tell my mother about our long plane ride, and why you didn't sleep at all."

"Mmm, I liked the plane. I had my own TV, so I played video games and watched movies."

Hal squeezed Mary's other hand. "Doesn't Tigger, I mean Rocket T, sound smart? Smarter than we were at his age, right Mary? You're lucky, Rocket T. When we were kids, we never got to ride on a plane with our own TV."

"Papa, can she really hear me?"

"All we can do is try, T-Man. Our voices are helping her brain waves, you know? Maybe we'll activate them, and she'll say something. It'll be like we have superpowers! What do you think, Mom? Mom, can you see us?"

***

The first-grader looked at his great-grandmother lying on the bed, her eyes open and staring into space. He wondered whether she's still breathing. He couldn't tell from her chest because she looked ... frozen. He shuddered. He had learned in school another way to check whether someone was still breathing, but there was no way he'd put his hand up to her nose.

"Papa," he asked his grandfather, "can we go now?"

"Come on, you're bored already?" The boy stood and nodded, but Papa remained seated.

"T-Man, let's talk to her some more. I think she can hear us. Look. Mom, can you hear us? If you can hear us, move your right hand."

To the boy's astonishment, his great-grandmother slowly focused her eyes on them and started inching her right hand, barely, back and forth.

"Oh, Mom, that's great! See that, Rocket? It's working. Mom, your great-grandson and I are here to keep you company. It's so great to be here with you. Just keep focusing on us and we'll keep telling you stories, all right? What's that, Mom?"

Her lips were moving and, without realizing it, the boy leaned in to try to hear what the old woman was trying to say.

"Hal." She didn't exactly say it; it was more like exhaling.

"I'm right here, Mary. Don't worry. I'm not going anywhere."

The boy sighed and sank into a chair.

Great-Grandpa Hal reached across the bed for the boy's hand. "Hey, Rocket T, want to hear a story? I want to tell you a story about how I met Mary. OK?"

"Mmm 'k."

"I first saw Mary at the big skating rink. My friends and I went about three nights a week. By this time, I was twenty-one and a half years old and looking for a wife. I wanted to get married young and have kids. I wanted two boys that could be like my brother and me. Bosom buddies. My brother was two years younger than me. We did everything together. We were dirt poor, but we had each other. I saw this new gal, white blouse and black skirt, poor skater. I asked her for the next skate. As we skated along, it was rough holding her up. But she seemed so clean, no makeup. After the skate, I took her back to where she was sitting and skated back to the other side of the rink to sit with my buddies. As I was sitting there, I saw her awkwardly come back over, looking for me. At the rink, they had three skates that were a lady's choice. You know what that is?"

Papa said, "Rocket, it's where the girl asks you to dance on skates with her. It used to be that usually boys ask girls to dance, not the other way around."

"She asked for the first lady's choice, but some other gal already asked me. How about second lady's choice, I had that; third lady's choice, I had that. I watched her struggle back to her seat. I felt sorry for her as she wasn't getting many skating partners. So at the last skate of the night, I figured I'd ask her. Next skating night, she was there again. I liked her clean looks and not-flashy clothes. I skated with her several times. It was an ordeal 'cause she couldn't skate very well and I'd have to hold her up around the rink. But I wanted to know more about her. She invited me to her house. She was the oldest of five kids. She treated her brothers and sisters, and her mother, so gently that I thought, 'Hey, maybe.' We started dating, and I just liked her quaintness and gentleness. The family was even poorer than mine. Her father was dead, and they struggled financially. My mom was dead set against us getting married. She said if Mary's mother died, I would struggle forever to feed and clothe her and her four siblings."

Papa said, "Your great-grandmother loved children, Rocket."

"Yeah, even before we moved to Colorado, we were foster parents in Davenport, Iowa. We didn't have a lot of money, but we ran a grocery store."

"You had a grocery store?"

"Yes, Rocket. It wasn't very big, but it had most things."

"Like candy? Toys?"

"All that good stuff. But we didn't make that much. I decided I needed to finish school, get a degree so I can make more money for my sons. That's what I did while Mary worked for a dry-goods store. We continued to be foster parents. That's how we came to adopt our daughter. And then after all our children were grown, Mary loved children so much, she started a daycare center. She took care of a lot of babies." Great-Grandpa Hal turned to Papa. "Say, how did I do, Bob? I wanted to tell that story at the ... at her service. That was good practice, don't you think?"

"Dad, don't."

"Heck, Bob, I was the one who taught you positive thinking. But I think she's determined to leave us. Her work here is done. She's ready to join her Maker. I think I'll ask them to play her favorite song at the service, *Just A Closer Walk with Thee*."

"Papa, are you crying?"

"It's OK ... I'm OK, Rocket T-Man. I'm all right."

***

She was lying on a frilly bed with her eyes closed. Her son couldn't describe it as sleeping because he didn't know. It wasn't as if he could ask her.

His grandson had gotten too restless sitting by the deathbed, so the man's father took the boy to lunch. If he had to guess, it was to his father's favorite restaurant, Old Country Buffet. The family ought to buy stock in the chain considering how often they ate there every time they visited Colorado.

He looked at his mother, breathing faintly. Above her head on a shelf were photographs he had sent from Indonesia, where his son was working for the U.S. Embassy and where they were living together in one house, three generations, just as they did outside Washington, D.C. He peered at the faces of his grandchildren in the photos, then back down at his mother. He was at a loss.

If she could still hear him, what would she want to hear? His mind raced through her letters to him about her early years, and then through his memories of his own early years. Awful, cold oatmeal, sometimes three times a day because they couldn't afford anything else. Her lack of affection. Odd for a woman who loved children so much. She did her duties, but there were no extras, no hugs and kisses, rarely an "I love you." At his mother-in-law's deathbed, didn't Carol Anne and her sister say the same thing about Nanny?

No. Think.

"Mom. Can you hear me?" Gently, he took one of her limp hands, the skin pale and losing its animal warmth. Or was it just how cold they kept the air conditioning in this building? Fighting back the urge to cringe, he wrapped both his hands around her frail one and tried to warm it up. Memories of other faces and other hands from his military days in the Vietnamese Mekong Delta — distant, ghostly, stinking with fear — hovered in the back of his mind.

He shook his head. This was about my mother. She had nothing to do with you.

He decided to test some words. "Remember that pastor at our church, Mom? I do." Nothing.

He exhaled, took a deep breath, and dove in again. "This was when I was thirteen or fourteen, maybe? He had a beautiful wife. I think she was a city woman, seemed unhappy all the time because her husband wanted to stay a preacher man in such an unsophisticated place. Wasn't what she had bargained for when she married him."

He took another breath. "She made his life miserable; everyone at church could see that. I did, though I was just a kid. So did you, Mom."

Maybe he should stop. She might be offended. He squeezed his mother's hand and then he couldn't help it, his eyes swelled with tears and he began to sob. He gasped and gasped until he could control his voice again. "You had such a rough life, Mom. Such an unhappy marriage with Dad for so long. The pastor obviously appreciated you. You idolized him and he ... he obviously appreciated being appreciated. You made him feel special."

Careful.

"I just want you to know, that's all, that I hope — I know this might sound strange coming from your son — but really, I really hope that you consummated your relationship with him. I don't mean to be disrespectful or anything, and I'm sorry, but you had it so rough, I wouldn't have blamed you at all. In fact, Mom, it would make me happy to think that you allowed yourself some happiness. All those years, sometimes you deserve something just for yourself. Mom? I'm not asking whether you did it. I'm not accusing you of anything. I love you, and I, I'm just saying I would understand. That's all."

He searched her face — his eyes, hands, and ears alert and hopeful for any movement or sound.

But his mother's shell gave away nothing.

**

It was a new day. Hal touched his ex-wife's cheek. He wondered whether she had awakened at all since last night. "Mary, we're back. We had to leave Rocket T at home with Vi today. He was too restless."

"Mom?"

"We had a good go of it, didn't we, Mary?"

Bob sighed. "Where are you planning on having the funeral?"

"The Lutheran Church she's belonged to all these years with John. I've already alerted the pastor. You want to say something at the service? You should think about it."

"Honestly, Dad, all I can think about is how she lived her whole life serving men. First you, then her ungrateful sons, then John. Mom? Mom, I'm real glad that in your last years you had people who waited on you here at the nursing home. I wish I could have done more for you, Mom."

"I feel real close to your mom right now. Don't you?"

"Yes. I do."

"You ever wonder what's next for her?"

Bob put his head in his hands. "Oh, you know that, like you, I don't believe in Heaven or Hell."

"Say, I sent Thuan an e-mail thanking her for letting their oldest son come all the way back here with you, letting Rocket go to the funeral. You know what she wrote me?"

Bob shrugged.

"That it's Rocket's duty to go to the funeral, that he has no right not to attend the service. She said it'll teach him about life and death. And she doesn't understand people saying funerals are not for the dead but for the living, as if it's a bad thing. I have to admit it's what I always thought. Didn't you? Funerals to me were always pretty useless, unnecessary expenses just to comfort the living. But that's not how Thuan sees it."

Bob looked up at him.

"Her e-mail said a funeral *is* for the living, as it should be. This is how each generation learns its place in the — how did she put it — the stream of time. Isn't that something what that little gal wrote me? Is that from her being raised a Buddhist?"

"I don't know that it's Buddhism. Thuan's mother is Buddhist, but not all Vietnamese are. Most of them worship ancestors. Even in America, many Vietnamese families have ancestral altars. We have one at our house with Thuan's dad on it and other relatives."

"Say, Bob, am I imagining this? Feel your mom's hand. It's stone cold."

"Mom?" Bob squeezed his mother's hand with both his own. "Should we call the doctor? Mom, can you feel my hand?"

Hal pressed a button on the wall. Then he stood and began murmuring, "Blessed are the dead who die in the Lord henceforth."

Bob stared at his father, questioning their shared atheism. "What are you doing?"

"Serving her last wishes. It's Revelation 14. Your mother wanted it printed in the program." Hal bent over to kiss Mary. "Honey, it's Hal. These are going to be my last words to you. I hope I can remember this correctly. Are you ready, sweet, gentle soul?

"Blessed indeed, says the Spirit, that they may rest from their labors, for their deeds follow them."

Mary Filipi died June 28, 2004. She was survived by two sisters and a brother. Attending her memorial worship service at Peace Lutheran Church in Arvada, Colorado, on July 1, were her first husband, two of their three children, two of their six grandchildren, one of their great-grandchildren, and many of her friends and fellow members of the church. At a later date, her ashes were taken to join those of her second husband, John Filipi, at Fort Logan National Cemetery.

Seven

When Grandma Mary passed away, I didn't really know her, though I had spent time with her.

It wasn't until half a decade later that I read her letters kept by my father-in-law, your Papa. I devoured all the details of her early life — from how much things cost, brewing beer during Prohibition, to Christmas presents of underwear made from bleached flour sacks.

I felt like a jerk that I never asked her the right questions when she was alive, so that now reading a dead woman's words I was surprised by how spunky your great-grandmother was as a girl, a girl who was beaten down by so many things out of her control yet who bravely passed into adulthood and found a way to reinvent herself, right until the end, several new Marys to astound the old.

About the time I was reading these letters of Daddy's paternal grandmother, he was leafing through ten thousand black-and-white and color photographs that both sides of our family had been saving, in boxes and bags and albums stored in the hut beneath our sunroom as well as in dark cabinets all over the house. Your father digitally scanned more than a thousand of them and eventually chose half of those for our family history photo book.

The images really brought home to me how your paternal great-grandmothers were nowhere close to living and dying in the same America. Nanny's world was straight out of *Mad Men*; Grandma Mary's Midwest would be considered mythically exotic by our Vietnamese side of the family. What the two American grandmothers shared was a country, a gender, and the Great Depression. That was it.

At times, yes, they suffered a similar hopelessness. Sometimes, as poet Barton Sutter wrote, "to live until we die — the job seems just impossible."

Life is a long time. A lot of abiding time and spending time. But also borrowed time. From whom are we borrowing it, those before us or after? Do we really owe our ancestors as well as our descendants? Who agreed on such a system? Who agreed on such words as honor, duty, love? Can't we ever live for just ourselves?

It was after Grandma Mary's death in 2004 that I started wondering about my husband's grandmothers and mine, comparing their cultures and choices. At the time, our family was living in Jakarta, Indonesia, where Daddy worked at the U.S. Embassy and you went to school with kids from all around the world.

My girl, my only daughter, you had just learned how to read. We were at a shopping mall cinema and you enunciated aloud a movie poster in English: "Live Your Life." I can still see you, five years old and pudgy, with chin-length hair and bangs framing your big eyes; I can still hear you declaring, "That should be live with your life!" And I remember thinking: Girl! Some day in the future when you're rebelling against whatever, I will remind you of today.

By then, Daddy's grandmothers were no more but mine were still living, one in Arizona and the other in Vietnam. Because Indonesia was so close, we took you children to visit Vietnam a couple of times, to our northern ancestral provinces and villages, and to the southern city where I was born.

Eight

NGUYEN, THI KIM (continued)

"Mother, the taxi is here."

"Who ... who's coming?"

"You don't have to sit up yet. Rest until I bring Thuan's family in."

"Thuan is coming? Tea ready?"

"Thuan's bringing her little ones to Viet Nam for the first time. I got some of those juice boxes my boss' children seem to like so much."

My youngest son, so considerate, finally engaged to be married. It helped that Thinh had a computer job, with a future, for a foreign company. But who knew whether I'll live long enough to go to his wedding, or meet another grandchild? I'm like a leaf on a quivering stem; a wind could part me from the branch any day now.

So fast. I turned around and it had already been a decade since Thuan and Bob lived in Sai Gon. Those couple of years, their family members also visited from America: Bob's parents, Thuan's sister and three brothers. Thuan brought them all here to see me. When her parents-in-law visited, oh, the neighbors still talked about it ... their hair, their eyes, what they wore, how much they smiled — all so foreign. I had expected that. What I had never expected was how

Thuan's younger siblings, also my paternal grandchildren, would be so foreign, too.

The strangest was the oldest of the three brothers. He looked exactly like their father. The square face, glasses, and intelligent eyes all reminded me of "Knowing Mind." This grandson, though dressed in shorts, kneeled and looked into my face. I tried to talk to him, but he kept staring at me, a quizzical smile on his lips. At first, I thought he was making fun of me, of my poverty. But those eyes, those eyes knew how to talk, and as I gradually understood what they were communicating ... thinking about it scared me all over again. It was his first time back to Viet Nam since he left as a little boy, and he was seeing me through the memories of what must have been to him a happy childhood. This grandson, really a man who might as well have been a stranger I had just met, was smiling at me with ... love. I'd never have imagined it. Politeness, respect, duty, yes. Anything but love.

At least Thuan's other siblings were foreign yet non-threatening. The second brother, whom we used to call "The Ant" because his head was bigger than his scrawny body, had grown into a tall man. So had the third brother. It was all that milk and nutrition Viet Nam didn't have. They looked like Japanese or South Korean tourists. The sister, the youngest of the five, was not as tall, but she also did not look Vietnamese. Curly hair; T-shirt and shorts.

Yes, foreign. Not resembling their parents or my husband at all. And none of those three youngest ones remembered me.

Which was a blessing. They had been too little when they left in '75. They had no memories of me and didn't expect anything from me, unlike Thuan and that first brother. And their mother.

Of course, Duc had been visiting me since Viet Nam opened up. While Thuan and Bob lived in Sai Gon a decade ago, Duc flew here a couple of times. Now, January 2004, she was with them on this trip, too. Yesterday, she came here by herself instead of waiting for the rest of the family. What a complicated woman! I thought I knew Duc ...

At least we had just managed to pay for the new roof and the new floor tiles. At least Thuan will walk through and see our lives have improved. Two bedrooms now, and a modern bathroom attached to the new kitchen. This was why my bed's back here, so I can be close to the bathroom. Not that I can make it there by myself anymore. My eyes aren't what they used to be, or my legs.

"Mother, here's Thuan and her family. Let me help you sit up."

"Uncle, we don't want to tire her."

"Is that you, granddaughter?"

"Yes, Ba Noi. My husband and I have brought our little ones to visit you. Oh, don't try to sit if you can't."

"It's all right; just lean me on this pillow. *HAO A U?*"

I could hardly see my grandson-in-law, but I heard him speaking his language to his children. "*Hey, guys, Great-Grandmother asked how are you — just like she asked me the first time I came here. What do you say?*"

"Chao Ba." "Chao Ba." "Chao Ba."

"Good, good children. I can't see well these days, so you have to come real close. I want to see your faces, all right?"

"*Come on, let's sit on the bed.*"

"*No, Daddy.*" "*Don't want to.*" "*I wanna stand.*"

"*Come on, guys, you can sit near her for just a minute.*"

"Mother, give them these chocolate candies."

Taking the tiny packages from Thinh, I held them out toward the tiny voices. "Be good. Want candy?" Good, good. Oh, such wee little hands, and I can just about make out your little eyes and tiny mouths. Look at them, frightened out of their minds to come so close to me, just like those little kids meeting a witch in those American books Thuan used to read.

But how could I fault them? Though Thinh dressed me in a silk blouse and my best-tailored pants, I know I must look scary. My sons had to cut off all my hair — almost a meter — because I can't take care of it anymore. Cropped head, arms and legs like sticks, I must resemble one of those Nazi concentration camp victims I've seen in history books.

"Ba Noi oi, how ... Uncle, what happened to her face?"

"She fell in the living room, hit her face on the edge of the coffee table. So that was it — we told her she can't move around by herself anymore. But niece, you shouldn't worry. When I'm at work, the daughters-in-law take turns sitting with her. *Don't worry, kids. Her face looks purple, but it doesn't hurt. The table did not hit her eye. Bob, do your children understand me?"*

"Oh, Uncle Thinh, your English is awesome."

"Thank you, Bob, and your Vietnamese accent is still very good. That's great. I thought that after you go back to America you will forget all you learned here."

"How can I forget? I live with Thuan's mother."

Thinh laughed. *"I know, but I was surprised to hear your parents have moved in with you, too! Thuan's mother was here yesterday and told us stories about what it's like living with American in-laws. Elder sister Duc cooks, your mother does laundry, your father even changes diapers! Ba Noi and I couldn't believe any American would agree to live the Asian way. You know, when you were still living in Viet Nam and your parents visited, I thought they were nice, but now from talking with elder sister Duc, I understand that they're really special. Thuan, your mother was here for a long time yesterday."*

Why was Thinh speaking so much English? "Thuan oi, come closer. Did you celebrate Christmas in Indonesia? That's where Uncle Thinh tells me you're living because of Bob's job. Do they celebrate Christmas there?"

"Ba, Christmas in a Muslim country is like Christmas here, more shopping than going to church. We found a fake Christmas tree, but the kids didn't need a real tree as long as there were a lot of toys underneath."

"Why didn't you wait until our Lunar New Year to bring your children to Viet Nam for the first time? Let them have a taste of Tet in their motherland. When was it you moved back to America?"

"1996. We lived in Sai Gon from 1994 to 1996."

"Why did you wait so long to come back?"

"It's the little ones, Ba. We were busy with your great-grandchildren."

"How old are they?"

"They're six, five, and three."

"Did you know, your father learned to play cards when he was just five?"

"Hey guys, she's telling me about my dad, and he learned to play cards when he was five!"

"Goldfish?" "Crazy Eight's not so hard." "Did he play War?"

"Your father was so smart. Cards, chess, Mahjong. And then there were the buses. Your father and his friends hung around the station and bothered the drivers all the time. Your Ong Noi used to complain about your father learning low-class slang. Then one day, a neighbor reported seeing your father learning to drive a bus. He was only twelve."

Thuan laughed. *"Bob, did you get all that? Isn't that hilarious?* Ba Noi, in America, you're not allowed to start learning to drive until you're fifteen. When I turned fifteen, my father insisted on teaching me in our *station wagon*, not as big as a bus, but it's a long car. My father said that once you can handle a big vehicle, driving smaller ones would be easy. Now I understand."

"And all that was even before I married your Ong Noi."

"Ah, yes. My father told me his mother died when he was thirteen or so."

"Did your father also teach you how to knit?"

"Knitting?"

"Yes, knitting. He must have learned that from his mother. 'Knowing Mind' knitted beautiful sweaters. So beautiful that when the family needed the money, I could actually sell ..." Oh Heaven! Why can't I hold my tongue anymore? I didn't mean to bring this up at all.

"Sell what, sweaters, Ba? Uncle, can you understand what she's saying?"

Why ask Thinh? He wasn't even born until after we fled the north.

All the older children had to help support the family once the Viet Minh started harassing my husband about his mandarin position in a French post office. Your grandfather's name was on a list of collaborators with the colonialist French, and the Viet Minh hunted them down like dogs. Our family began running from the enemy.

"Your Ong Noi had to change our family name in 1951, from Nguyen to Le. Did your father ever tell you about that, when your grandfather Nguyen Van Hai became Le Tat Tien?"

"Yes, Ba, this I do know. But it was my mother who told us my father's family name was once Nguyen, like hers and yours, Ba Noi, not Le. When I asked my father, he stressed he wanted us to forget it and not tell anybody. I thought he was still carrying that fear of being discovered, even all the way in America. But he told us this name change was so long ago that it didn't matter. He said it was so long ago, he had ceased to think of himself as a Nguyen. He preferred to think of himself as a Le because the Le emperors chased the Chinese out and established Vietnamese laws and culture. He really identified with and felt sorry for the last Le king."

"Just like your father to always be the sentimental, dutiful one." When I became his mother, I was only twenty-five. All my husband's sons tried to please me. Once I had children of my own, I told the stepsons that to care for their little brothers and sisters was to show their respect for me.

Running from the enemy.

You couldn't trust anyone. That was just a fact of life for as long as the Viet Minh and the French were fighting it out. There were Viet Minh zones where the French wouldn't dare enter and, suddenly, our Thanh-Hoa Province was one of those zones. My husband didn't even notice! He was too busy with cards and cronies.

A mandarin somewhere nearby would get his throat slit, or a

French government building would be burned to the ground, and we would go into hiding for a week, sometimes months, in the countryside, and then the French forces and the Vietnamese colonial soldiers would pacify Thanh-Hoa Province, and we'd return home thinking that was the end of that. But then the Viet Minh would come into Thanh-Hoa again in the middle of the night, and we'd pack up all the children again and go to some other province until it was safe to go back home. Just imagine living like that, the future uncertain.

What was incredible was that each time we were back safely at home, it would seem a long time and we'd forget to worry. War seemed so far away from the everyday running of the house. What did the name of the ruler of Viet Nam have anything to do with anything when a child had a burning fever and we had to call the doctor, or when a nursemaid was so sick she couldn't breastfeed the baby? Children needed basic things, whether they were mine or his. A home, food, education.

***

A shadow flickered in a corner of the kitchen, and Madame Kim instinctively shuddered.

Who's there?

She turned toward the new presence in the room. Her eyes widened. Breathe, she told herself. Stay calm. *How, Madame, how did you slip in here without anyone noticing? Look, literally look, I can see! Heaven, my nearly blind eyes can suddenly really see you there, Madame — hair coiled around your head just like the old traditional way, your face so young and white against your dark tunic. That face ... so familiar ...*

This can't be. *Have we met? Perhaps when we were both maidens? How is it I can see you standing there as clear as day while those sitting around me are so blurry?*

Are you who I think you are? Why do you suddenly appear now? Is it my time? But I'm not ready! Can't you see I'm busy? I can't go until

*Thuan understands me. Once she understands, Madame, you will under-
stand. Madame, I swear to you, please have mercy.*

***

"Thuan? Granddaughter, where are you?"

"I'm here, Ba Noi. I'm holding your hands."

Keep your voice calm. "You have to tell your children stories
about your father as I'm telling them to you. Will you remember?
Where are the little ones? Are they still in the room?"

"Ba Noi, don't tire yourself."

"Truth be told, your father's eldest brother followed the Viet
Minh. Apologize to your American husband for me. Bob's father
was a soldier in the war against communism, but when your eldest
uncle joined the Viet Minh, they weren't communist yet. Even your
father and the younger boys wanted to follow them. No Vietnamese
wanted to be ruled by a foreign power; everybody thought Ho Chi
Minh was leading a bunch of nationalist boy scouts. But sooner or
later, the Viet Minh showed their true nature. By then, we could no
longer communicate with your eldest uncle.

"Your father and his younger brothers were very smart. They
knew not only Vietnamese but also Mandarin and French. Because
of the Viet Minh chasing your grandfather, his post office job was
unstable. Do you understand? Can you make your children understand? Use simple words."

"Ba Noi, there's no need to rush."

But there is! Child, you don't see that white-face woman standing in the corner of the room. Yesterday, I told these stories to your
mom when she visited, but I want you to hear it directly from my
mouth. I don't understand your mother anymore. Duc has changed,
softer, kind. Actually, yesterday, Duc fed me. When she spoke, Duc
was — and truly I couldn't have expected this — full of compassion.
But who knows? In the future, her heart can change again, so I still
want to explain to you myself why I did what I did.

"Ong Noi placed the older sons with families deep in the villages where they'd be safe. Your father and uncles lived with rich landowners who wanted live-in tutors for their sons. They were allowed to continue to go to school; every month they got paid. But your father and his brothers were such good sons that each month, they'd come home and give your Ong Noi their salaries so we could take care of their little brothers and sisters. No one forced them. Same with the sweaters your father knitted. No one forced him to knit them. But people liked buying them."

Don't look at me like that. Everything was suddenly clear to me — your children's eyes — tell them to stop staring at me. It's as if these little ones knew that once upon a time, my stepsons had to share one pair of dress pants among them. It's as if they knew that my stepsons had to walk several kilometers just to see each other and ten kilometers to go to school. I didn't have brothers or sisters. I didn't know siblings could love one another as much as my stepchildren did. Each would think nothing of walking to visit the others. For major exam days, whoever needed those dress pants would have to walk all those kilometers to get them from whoever wore them last.

"My father already told me this, Ba."

Holy hell! Had I been talking out loud this whole time? "Granddaughter, what did you say?"

"My father said that to go to school, he had to walk a long way, through mud and rice paddies, and barefoot. My father said it was funny thinking back about it. He and the uncles didn't see it as suffering at all and were even delighted to feel the mud between their toes. My father said that while walking from one green rice paddy after another, he used to recite classical poetry to himself or make up his own verses."

"Your father said what?"

"Ba, that first year we came to America as refugees, after a few months my father passed the driver's license test. A person from the Lutheran church that sponsored us gave my father an old car, and another church person helped him find a job. The car didn't have air conditioning or heat. Ba Noi, the state of Arizona is in the American desert, like in the cowboy movies. Summer is hot enough to fry an egg on the sidewalk, but winter is very cold. Going to work, my father wore a thick jacket and exhaled cold smoke from his mouth. My father said winters in Arizona couldn't compare with the wind that blew in northern Viet Nam. He said that when he was growing up, there was no central heating to fight those piercing northern winds. He told us we had to realize how lucky we were to be in America."

Correct! That's what I'm trying to tell you. I paid for all his past suffering by not going to America. Don't you see? Whatever sins you think I committed, they were out of love for my children. You can't reproach a mother for that. And look what happened? Heaven already struck me. Our family didn't listen to Nghia that night in '75. We didn't go to America. All these years, don't you think I and your aunts and uncles have suffered enough? Let it end with my death and spare my children's children. "You there, standing in the corner so quietly. Madame, did you hear me?"

"Uncle, who is she talking to? Ba Noi, lie down. You're scaring the kids."

"Did your father tell you — come closer — his oldest brother stayed back in North Viet Nam. Our family left in '54. Your eldest uncle was the only one who stayed."

"I know."

"I didn't make him stay back. The Viet Minh did. You can't put that blame on my head. But I'm trying to make it up to him now. He must have married and had children. I told your mother when she was here yesterday. I said she had to go out north to find your uncle and remind him that I didn't make him stay. Help him. Tell him I sent you so some of the karma will rub off on me, too."

"Uncle Thinh, could you take my husband and children to the front room? Please let them light incense at the altar."

"Bob, I'm sorry. Ba Noi is like this all the time now. We keep telling her the past doesn't matter. Nobody cares anymore. It's just the past."

If I have to be reincarnated, as the Buddha teaches, please have mercy and don't let it be something bad. Let me stay in the family so I can still be tied to my loved ones and meet my future great-grandchildren. "Would that be all right, Madame?"

"Ba, who are you talking to?"

The woman in the shadows flickered like a candle. Her eyes brightened and her mouth curved into a smile full of ... ah, Madame, now I understand. "Thuan, I'm sorry if I scared you. I thought that woman came back to get me, but maybe she's just here to see you."

"What did my mom say to you yesterday to scare you like this? I apologize, Ba, if she said anything to upset you. Ba Noi, can you hear me?"

Nguyen Thi Nhuan. Is that you? My predecessor, the real Ba Noi to granddaughter Thuan? But of course, she looks exactly like you, that perfectly round face. Blood doesn't lie. I beg of you to come out from that corner and take a good look at our granddaughter. Are those the clothes you were buried in? How does this work?

You're smiling. Well, what do you have to complain about? One of your sons made it all the way to America, and his eldest daughter is sitting here next to me. Look at her children in the front room, their eyes not complete almonds and their hair not black. Go, take a good look at them. Follow your bloodline. They'll be leaving Viet Nam soon and you won't ... Heaven, I forget! What does travel mean to you anymore? A woman who died on a boat and who had never even been in an automobile while you were alive, certainly you now couldn't care less about that thing we call an airplane. I suppose you can fly around by yourself. What a laugh that I should worry about you! I suppose you can follow our descendants anywhere you want. Come to think of it, I suppose I soon can, too.

***

Madame, you're still here. The house feels so empty. Has everyone forgotten us? You're so kind to sit with me like this. I'm not at peace. My story is ending, and I'm not at peace. You couldn't have been, either, when your life ended so early. Our days are gone.

Our great-grandchildren — remember when half-breeds were shameful? They were to be hidden, or their mixed bloodline needed to be hidden. They had to pass for Vietnamese. But that was in our days, and our days are gone.

I respectfully plead with you, elder sister Nhuan: Haven't I been punished enough? Yet Thuan's mother insists on torturing me. She's so kind. My stepdaughter-in-law has turned out to be so merciful. I thought for sure after Nghia died that she'd no longer send money back to Viet Nam for us, that she'd cut us off and tell her children to forget us. I was so sure about this that, to stay a step ahead, I started writing letters directly to Thuan. I thought that this granddaughter would be like her father, sentimental, dutiful. But Thuan's mother has proved that she was one step ahead of me the whole time, that all my worrying was for naught. Her family's financial aid to ours continues to this day, and though Nghia is no longer alive, Duc still tried to sponsor me, my children, and grandchildren to America. It was America and its immigration technicalities that turned us down, not Duc.

Yes, Duc has been full of tricks, full of surprises. She has become a woman full of mercy. I thought she would hand that mercy out with relish, as punishment. But no. And, Madame, elder sister Nhuan, could you please explain this to me? Because I'm still trying to understand why.

Nguyen Thi Kim died October 31, 2004. A stepson (the sole survivor out of four), her four sons and their wives, a son-in-law, and all their children led the funeral procession to her final resting place in Thu Duc, Viet Nam.

Nine

Once we returned to live in America in 2005, we took you children to visit my mother's mother in a Phoenix suburb. She was in her late eighties by then. My sister, living nearby with her family and much more familiar with our grandmother, said, "I don't know why you bother. You know Ba Ngoai won't even remember who you are, right?" I thought to myself, I'm not doing this for Ba Ngoai; I'm doing this for my kids.

Now I know better.

Just like our visits to Ba Noi in Vietnam and to Grandma Mary in Colorado, taking you kids to see Ba Ngoai in Arizona wasn't for your benefit. If it weren't for family albums, none of you would even remember being in the same room with any of these women, these photographed souls who are intimately a part of you, a part of me. I guess that each time, with each grandmother, I needed to see my past and my future in one place, my personal story on one page.

My story is not finished; neither is yours. How will we end?

Ten

VU, THI TY
(born in 1918)

She straightened her bifocals and leaned forward, trying to see how the black-and-white man's name was spelled on TV. "Ba Rack, Ba Rack," Madame Ty whispered to herself. She paused to listen to how the American reporters said his family name, then tried it, "O Ba Ma. O Ba Ma."

Not that this U.S. senior citizen via Viet Nam could understand the rest of what the reporters were saying. She just liked looking at all the replays of the man and his Jackie Kennedy-esque wife. Vietnamese newspapers in America had been full of photographs and stories about this couple — his black Kenyan father and white American mother; her bloodline from Southern plantation slaves, probably even from the plantation owners. "And from those beginnings," Madame Ty mumbled, "now you'll sit on high."

On the screen, young versions of the black-and-white man appeared over a long string of words, of which the only one Madame Ty recognized was "Honolulu."

I lived there. When I first came to America in '75, I lived in Honolulu with my daughter Nancy and her husband, Warren Tanita. Of course, Nancy was not the name her father and I gave her.

Hòa (agreement, peace) changed her name to Nancy after meeting Warren, a Japanese American soldier stationed in Viet Nam who, when his tour was done, brought her back with him to Hawaii.

It's a small island, Madame Ty remembered, so I might have seen this Ba Rack boy around Honolulu. Wonder when he left? When did I leave Hawaii for Arizona? I forgot. Why did I leave?

Madame Ty lifted her head to lower the bifocals as her eyes wandered to the brand new president's ears. Buddha ears, she noted. Good long lobes. And nothing pinched about this face. Wide nostrils and mouth, a sign of generous times coming for the country. Well, it couldn't come soon enough. In our family alone there were too many layoffs.

The TV people kept showing his name, perhaps just to get the whole country used to it. All the stations had been replaying his campaign appearances from last year and from Election Day.

Madame Ty cleared her throat and, without taking her eyes off the screen, called out, "Toan, did you take me to go vote for O Ba Ma?"

The woman in the kitchen said without stopping her chopping: "His inauguration is only a few days away. Do you understand, Mother, that America is getting its first black president? Today is, what, Saturday? He'll be sworn in Tuesday."

Then I'll really have seen everything, Madame Ty smirked at herself.

Her daughter continued, "If they could only wait a week — less than a week — Mother just think, then he could be inaugurated right on Tet. The 26th of January. That would truly be auspicious."

"What did you say about Tet?" Lunar New Year was here? Madame

Ty was horrified she's unprepared, like that nightmare in which the elite boys' school finally allowed her in but she left all her books at home.

"Mother, have faith in me. Everything will be ready for the family altar on New Year's Eve."

"I'm going to lie down." All that squinting had tired Madame Ty's eyes. She put down her glasses and pushed herself slowly from the sofa. "Call me when dinner's ready."

***

"Mother?"

No response. Toan entered the room, sat gingerly on the bed, and leaned in closer to the old woman's face. Alarmed, she lifted her fingers toward her mother's nose and mouth, waiting for that puff of exhaled air, no matter how faint. Nothing. She tried to calm herself, like they teach you at the Red Cross class, as she felt her mother's neck and wrists.

She sat back. No more mother. No more making food for a toothless mouth. No more washing elderly underpants after accidents. All gone in an instant, with no big, painful, agonizing warning. Have to admit, Mother was as blessed in death as she was in life.

The woman hadn't been taking care of her mother long, only a couple of years. Before that, her youngest sister's family lived with Mother, for two decades or so, even after Mother became a handful, seeing visions and accusing people of all sorts of crazy things.

Nights were really bad. She'd go into the bathrooms and flush the toilets all the time. Or she'd look in the mirror and talk to relatives who've been dead and long gone. Sometimes she'd curse at the mirror, using words so foul she'd shock even her sons. Youngest sister, her husband, and their two children loved Mother, so they suffered through the nights because Mother was able to take care of herself during the day while they were at work or school. But once Mother needed someone to watch her all day, daughters and sons gathered for a big meeting, and out of the fifteen children, the eleventh said she would be the full-time caregiver.

Caregiver no more. Toan — a mother of grown children and a new grandmother herself — returned to the kitchen in a daze. She lifted the phone and speed dialed one of her older sisters. "Elder sister Nine? I think Mother is gone."

"When?"

"Just now."

"You dial 911. I'll call everyone."

"I need to call 911?"

"Just do it. Was she in any pain? Did she say anything?"

"She went to lie down and told me to wake her for dinner. That's it."

Sigh. "Call 911. I'll call the family."

While the emergency medics rolled up to the house outside Phoenix, while they confirmed the death of the woman whose family name was Vu and whose first name was Ty (pronounced TEE, the daughter informed them), the clan's phone tree spread the news all around Arizona's Valley of the Sun, up and down California, through the Pacific to Hawaii, and overland across the width of America east to Virginia. Until all the matriarch's descendants had been alerted.

**

Madame Ty impatiently played with her jade bracelet and smoothed out her silk velvet ao dai. She looked around for her husband. Where did he go? He was about to introduce me to some people, but suddenly he's gone and I'm standing here next to this tall boy. Something about his face reminded me of a child I once knew, but I didn't know this tall boy with spiky hair and glasses at all.

"Cuz, tell me something," the boy said to a woman who's only as tall as his shoulder, "why did Ba Ngoai call our parents, her own children, miss this and uncle that, even referring to them as elder sister or elder brother?"

"Ba Ngoai belonged to a more formal world," the woman answered.

"Once you became an adult, people didn't call you by just your first name, not without a title of some kind. Not even your own parents. Not even your own spouse. Am I glad that tradition ended with her generation! Can you imagine your parents calling you Elder Brother Tony? Or my mom calling me Miss Quynh?"

The boy laughed. "I know, right?"

Out of nowhere, Mr. Tai reappeared. "Sir, where did you go? Why are there so many people?"

My husband's eyes turned to me. "Well, they're all here for you."

"But what is this occasion? I'm so confused. People aren't dressed in serious clothes, but it feels so serious, so very heavy."

Except on the other side of the room, where a lot of young people in jeans and sweaters were sitting in the pews or standing around, forty-somethings all the way down to toddlers. Whatever the reason for this grave reunion, they couldn't hide their joy at seeing one another again. There was a lot of hugging, back slapping, and hand shaking. Mingling among the Vietnamese were others whose skin tones ranged from brown to white, some with curly hair and some blond.

"Mr. Tai, do you know that young crowd over there? Should I know them?"

"Madame, look over here. Now do you recognize anyone?" His hand indicated the first few pews closer to us, where bespectacled elders sat according to age. The oldest were in the front row with their gray heads and stooped backs; behind them were several rows of men and women with thinning hair and sad, wrinkled smiles.

"Ah! Yes that's ..." But I didn't know whom to identify first because all their names instantaneously filled my head. There were my husband's two daughters by his first wife, and there was our firstborn, and the second, and the next and ... "Heaven. When did they get such hollow cheeks?" Unlike Mr. Tai. "How is it that you look younger than many of our children?"

"Miss, so do you."

He waved at a big mirror in a corner, and as we approached it together, I saw my eyes widening in disbelief. Except that my eyes are not staring out from the wrinkled face I had been seeing in the mirror these past decades. He and I ... it was like reliving the day we got married: Decked in gold and jade, I was in my traditional dark velvet ao dai over white satin pants, my hair (still black!) wrapped into a black velvet halo. As for Mr. Tai, no traditional ao dai and turban for him! He was wearing the black tuxedo made by the best French tailor in Ha Noi, with cuff links sent all the way from Paris.

Before I could ask Mr. Tai why we were wearing our wedding fineries again, the audience became silent and someone was speaking into a microphone.

"Who was Vu Thi Ty?" asked the woman at the podium. "She was Ba Ngoai to me and many of you in this room because our mothers were her daughters. But others here knew her as Ba Noi because your fathers were her sons. Here, I'll just call her our grandmother."

She took a deep breath. "We've heard a lot about our grandmother today: daughter of bookstore owners, sister to an iconic author, mother of fifteen, businesswoman, benefactor to those less fortunate. But here's something rarely mentioned: Our grandmother, at one point in Ha Noi, sold opium."

"What!" Laughter cut into the somber atmosphere from the young side of the room. The speaker scanned the audience, grinning. Even on this side of the room, though some elders frowned in disapproval, others smiled and shook their heads.

"Well, it wasn't illegal then under the French," the speaker continued. "I mean, opium was like aspirin under the French. Our grandparents had several businesses in Ha Noi — the Savonta soap factory, a trucking delivery service, houses for rent — but they also bought opium wholesale from traders going back and forth to southern China. They'd buy a big chunk and put it in some back closet. And when the household needed grocery money, our grandmother would scoop off a block to sell to local opium lounges."

As the woman spoke, I had been moving over to listen in on the young people: "A drug runner!" "For grocery money?" "I love it!" "OMG."

Somebody whispered, "Wait, like in that movie *China Town*?" "No, goofball, not Los Angeles! This was Viet Nam, like in *Indochine*."

A little boy asked, "What did they list on her death certificate?"

"Ba Ngoai died of plain old age, Cuz," answered the spiky-haired, tall boy from earlier. "She used to live with me, and I saw her aging as I was growing up. Trust me. It ain't fun. Her mind's been gone for years. Her body just decided it was time to catch up."

***

That was it then? That was why I suddenly can understand English?

Before I could reach out to try to touch this tall boy, to ask him for confirmation face to face, my husband stopped my arm.

I waited for Mr. Tai to say something, but he was avoiding my eyes. His eyes were shy, a word I wouldn't have used to describe him while he was alive. "Why so tongue-tied all of a sudden, Sir? Or don't you understand what I'm saying? What language am I speaking?"

His eyes fled from mine and darted toward the front of the room, beyond the speaker at the podium still telling tales of my life. There was an altar overflowing with candles, incense, fruit. Nearby were stands holding up huge wreaths of flowers slashed diagonally with ribbons. And at the center of the wall, there was an open casket.

I was gliding. There was no other word for it. I wasn't flying; it was just that I couldn't feel my feet, but I was moving toward the long box lined with satin. I looked into the casket and saw white, short hair; a leathery face smoothed out by the mortician's chemicals and made up with a heavy foundation; a golden, brocade ao dai; and my closed eyes. "Not bad, for a corpse."

Mr. Tai threw his head back and laughed. "Madame, I forgot your sneaky sense of humor. Not bad for a corpse! Look at you, there's that sly smile that always cheered me up."

Oh, why did the pleasure in his eyes give me so much satisfaction? How I had missed this dashing, gregarious man whom I hadn't seen since his funeral in 1962. Why did his eyes keep dancing around everything except what's in the casket? "Sir, are you afraid of looking at me?"

"But I *am* looking at you." He took my hands — in public — something he never used to do. "A chrysanthemum, like how I remember you."

Let go of my hands. "Mr. Tai, turn your head, look at this ninety-year-old thing no longer living. This is me now. The way you never had to age because you died from booze at fifty-three and left me with nothing but our children."

That did it. That wiped the smile off his face. "Is it my fault that monster Ho Chi Minh took over the north and we had to flee south and lost everything? Don't ... we have an eternity now. Where are you going?"

Don't, don't look back.

"But this is your wake. Tomorrow is the funeral, and Sunday there's a service at the temple. Madame, where are you going?"

***

When was the last time she saw Ha Noi?

Ha Noi, the capital city in the river's bend. Ha Noi and its poetic bodies of water. The central one, Hoan Kiem Lake, bordered the Old Quarter with its thirty-six tiny districts full of winding streets and families living over their shops. Look at the road signs, still named after whatever predominant commodity used to be sold in each district — silver, chicken, salt, coffin, drum, coal, silk ... She stopped, realizing that she really was looking at a street sign reading Pho Hang Gai. Around her, the silk merchants were just opening their stores, but the breakfast vendors already had been busy, some selling food from baskets and others from carts.

I'm back! Golden euphoria washed over her. Everything was as it should be on this street where she was born. Agreed, the merchants and the vendors weren't the same people she grew up with, and they had on just shirts and pants — lots of jeans even — and not the traditional ao dai everybody used to wear. Agreed, the dusty street had been paved over, and on it are 21st century cars and motorcycles instead of those old rickshaws pulled by men, carriages pulled by horses, and black automobiles pulled by unseen French engines. Even so, the street hadn't been widened into some behemoth boulevard, and the neighborhood still had an intimate feel to it. It was just more crowded and a lot noisier with the car engines and all the honking. On the other hand, she didn't miss one bit the smell of human urine or the sight of horse feces.

She tried to reorient herself, looking at the numbers on the shops — 115 Pho Hang Gai was around here somewhere. She glanced at the people walking past her. You'd think that a woman dressed from head to toe in old-fashioned finery, not to mention covered in gold and jade, would get stares this early in the morning. But no. No one was looking back at her. Out of curiosity, she stopped right where she was on the sidewalk.

And was rewarded by having several people walk right through her body.

She laughed, her hand covering her teeth. I'm a ghost, she thought. Then she said it out loud, "I'm a spirit haunting my old street!" No one answered. Every man, woman, and child who crossed her path or passed through her continued as if she didn't exist.

On a whim, she stepped into traffic on the narrow road, right in front of a yellow taxi. The driver didn't even blink as his car rolled into her front and out her back, and she ... she didn't feel a thing. Not the metal, not its weight, not its motion. Not even the life force of the old driver.

Vu Thi Ty froze with fear. A van rumbled through her, then a man pedaling a three-wheel cyclo taxi, then a roaring motorcycle. The self-preservation instinct belonging to all life forms was screaming at her to move to safety, an old habit refusing to face the new reality. But the fear gripping her had nothing to do with that life instinct or with the heavy metal vehicles coming straight at her without stopping.

Where *am* I going?

She looked around the street, scanned the sidewalks on both sides, and peered into the morning shadows. Could I now see deities? Were you coming for me? What was it going to be, Heaven or Hell?

Nothing. Nothing but mortals just going about their business, not paying attention to her at all.

Ha! Guess it wasn't time yet. She shook her head and glided back onto the sidewalk. Enough of that. Until whatever comes comes, you're looking for 115 Pho Hang Gai. She read the shop signs. Not the art gallery. Not that Asian-Western restaurant. Posters everywhere either wished customers a Happy New Year or advertised Tet sales. Wait, here.

"This is it," she mumbled. This was the address where she was born and where she lived until she married Nguyen Huu Tai. The narrow, long building still had two stories.

Of course, the sign above the door didn't say Book Store Quang Thinh anymore. It was now a boutique with clothes hanging in the doorway. And look, the top floor had windows now! The inside upstairs must be a lot brighter than the dark rooms of her youth. What must that be like? Was there anyone up there now? What must they be like? Anything like us?

As soon as our family's four boys and four girls could read, my siblings and I had to help out with the book shop downstairs, even the youngest, the one called Tiny by her future husband. In fact, the nickname was so fitting that even after she had children, she was known as Madame Tiny. *Ba Be.*

* * *

Madame Ty looked at her birthplace with wonder. So many souls with so many lives. Even this building. She stared past the hanging dresses in the doorway into the front room, remembering how the bookstore used to be, how she used to be. Did I get married first, or did my baby sister?

What ancient history, when no respectable adult kept his or her teeth the ivory color babies are born with. As soon as you became of age, you had your teeth lacquered until they turned the appropriate glossy ebony, and you started chewing betel nuts to help maintain the color. It was unbelievable how fast you got used to that jumpy feeling of the betel juice. I had heard it compared to caffeine, but I never drank coffee so I wouldn't know. What I *do* know is I used to look forward to how each betel nut chew made me feel — both more alert and relaxed.

Preparing the specialty was an art in itself. In fact, it was an art that would-be brides had to perform in front of prospective in-laws. At the appointed audition, the man's parents came to the maiden's house, then after some conversation, her parents called the damsel into the room. She'd stand there to be looked over from head to toe. Not that she could look back at anyone. Oh no, eyes down. Then when her parents asked her to, she'd kneel to prepare the betel nuts for the old people to chew.

I can still do this in my sleep. Hold the betel pepper leaf in your palm, spread a bit of lime on it, then place part of the betel nut in the middle and roll the whole thing. A maiden was graded for speed, neatness, proportions, and the shape of the roll. My mouth's watering just thinking about biting through the soft leaf and the sticky lime into the crunchy nut, then waiting for the glow that fired up and soothed your insides all at once.

Heaven, my last taste of betel nut was forever ago — 1975! I had to quit just like that when we fled Sai Gon. My children told me you didn't chew betel nuts in America, and you couldn't have black teeth in America. And now! Sigh. If I knew my last chew was really my last chew ...

Once upon a time, men and women who weren't related or wedded to each other rarely talked face to face. Once upon a time, people married in their late teens because that was adulthood, couples were expected to be grandparents by their forties, and no one would have been surprised if someone died in their fifties.

Once upon a time was not a fairy tale. Just as black teeth used to be fashionable, once upon a time was the norm.

But once upon a time, Madame Ty reminded herself, you were abnormal. You liked working in the bookstore and soon learned to run the shop. You and your sisters didn't receive much higher education; the elders sent only their sons to the French lycées and colleges in Ha Noi.

You, not to boast or anything, you had a talent for business. You liked the numbers coming into the store and you learned to manage the numbers going out. Mother and Father could count on you. Which was fortunate because they couldn't always count on every one of their eight children.

***

One of my brothers, Vu Bang, fell into poetry and fiction by age twelve, after reading all the Vietnamese, Chinese, and French books he was supposed to be selling in our family shop. From there, it was on to drinks and opium, then writing and journalism. I can't remember whether he even graduated from Lycée Albert Sarraut.

I certainly never had a chance to attend that most prestigious high school in Ha Noi; my family was conservative on how much to educate daughters. But among my brother's classmates was a girl named Tran Le Xuan, who later would marry a man named Ngo Dinh Nhu. In 1955, a year after the Geneva accords split Viet Nam in two and we were among a million people who fled south to escape communism, Nhu's brother Ngo Dinh Diem would defeat Emperor Bao Dai in a vote and ascend to become the president of the newly created "Viet Nam Cong Hoa," known in English as South Vietnam.

President Diem never married and lived instead like a priest, deeply committed to his Roman Catholic Church. He even had an older brother who was a bishop.

My brother's classmate Xuan, now known as Madame Ngo Dinh Nhu, moved with her husband into the presidential palace and was the de facto first lady. Really, truly, she and her husband ran South Vietnam. They were responsible for a lot of new laws, crackdowns on everything from freedom of the press to moral conduct. That whole Catholic family waged what amounted to a war against the Buddhist leaders. Here the people thought we were done with the Nguyen dynasty and kings forever, and instead we got the Ngo Dynasty. President Diem even appointed Madame Nhu's father — his sister-in-law's father — ambassador to the United States.

I never said this out loud to anyone, not in all these decades, least of all to my children because they would have called me crazy behind my back, but I knew who really killed President John F. Kennedy. It was all in the numbers.

Just think back to 1963: The Ngo regime sent troops to shoot at Buddhist demonstrators, then a prominent, respected monk burned himself alive on a busy street to denounce President Diem and his family's violations of human rights. That was how desperate things were. And we thought we had fled North Vietnam to get away from oppression.

What I remember was that by then, you didn't have to be a Buddhist, a communist, or a journalist to rebel against the South Vietnamese government. Even businesspeople like me thought the Ngo regime had to end. But the Ngos wouldn't leave; they were so powerful that even the Americans couldn't control them. On the other hand, the Ngos' underlings, tired of the corruption and the crackdowns on the people, must have let the Americans know they were ready to do their part.

South Vietnamese generals staged a coup on November 1. The very next day, President Diem and his brother Nhu were found shot to death in a church.

If you were the power-drunken Madame Nhu, infuriated and threatened by the assassination of your husband and your brother-in-law, what would you do? Well, yes, first you'd flee to France; people used to snicker that she was more fluent in French than she was in Vietnamese anyway. But then what? Wouldn't you want to teach somebody a lesson?

Twenty days later, JFK was assassinated. Think about that number; that wasn't even a month. Yet even now, Americans are still investigating who killed President Kennedy. Well, it's still a mystery because everyone's been looking in all the wrong places.

I bet brother Vu Bang would have agreed with me. In memoirs written in his old age, he recalled how devious Madame Nhu was even as a schoolgirl, and he lamented how one family failed the entire country and how individual decisions damned countless lives. He wrote all this in his Sai Gon days. In what was then our future. A future that's now my past.

Back in my brother's twenties, back here in Ha Noi, Vu Bang was one of the founders of a satirical magazine that made fun of not only the French, but also the Vietnamese elite whose power was loaned to them by the colonialists. A very noble enterprise, except he and his colleagues barely broke even with advertising. I caught him stealing stationery products from our Quang Thinh bookstore here on Pho Hang Gai, as well as ink and huge bulks of paper from the Quang Te printing press our family also owned on ... Where was it?

Oh, Madame Ty, how could you forget Kham Thien Street? It was where your brother became very intimate with its many ... musical houses, where singing girls learned how to wear makeup and how to play the 16-string dan tranh as part of their education in ... entertaining gentlemen.

Well, yes, we'd get angry with brother Vu Bang, and the old people would scold him, but really, I have to say we were secretly proud of him. When one magazine failed or another's publisher got arrested by the French, my brother and his friends would think nothing of creating another publication — be it satirical, investigative, or cultural. They wouldn't let any police forces, Vietnamese or foreign, intimidate them.

＊＊＊

As for our baby sister, she liked anything new and modern.

One day, someone ran into the bookstore yelling to my parents, "Madame, Sir, youngest miss is riding a bicycle around Hoan Kiem Lake!"

The family was horrified: A girl almost marriage age spreading her legs around a modern, Western contraption for all of society to see? What respectable family would want her for a bride after that? Just imagine, then, our parents' faces on another day when she came home with her long hair — which I had been patiently teaching my baby sister to wrap into a black velvet crown appropriate for her age and station

— cut off to her chin and permed into waves, just like on the French dames.

**

Whatever our elders' fears, they needn't have worried about their youngest finding a husband. She would marry and have children and grandchildren.

You, on the other hand, Madame Ty told her former self, relatives and friends would introduce young men to you and you couldn't be bothered. Maybe the men were too young. And really, you were too busy with the family businesses. Then somebody brought Mr. Tai to the house, and the parents encouraged you to meet him. "Daughter, you'd like him," they said. "He's a manager at a company that sells paper and oil."

And the elders were right. That time, it was different.

If Nguyen Huu Tai were a book, Madame Ty chuckled, I suppose I fell in love with the cover. What did I know? I didn't have time to do much research, so I followed traditions and let the family choose. And he *did* look good on paper: A gentleman of position with family roots in Hanh-Thien, a village renowned for producing scholars and mandarins. Mr. Tai was among the fourteenth generation of descendants from Nguyen Thien Sy, who in 1522 became the minister of education at the court of the Le dynasty. Mr. Tai's own father was the chief of a government district.

Mr. Tai also had been married to a woman from Hanh-Thien, but she died of illness several years before I met him. This first wife had given him young daughters who now needed a mother.

I supposed my heart went out to a widower raising his little girls. I certainly felt I would be his match on the business side and, despite the fact that my family didn't believe in educating girls, I was confident I could hold my own on the intellectual side as well. After all, brother Vu Bang wasn't the only sibling to have read the Vietnamese books in the family store before they were sold. As I said, all the children were expected to help out, even with the customer recommendation lists on history, religion, poetry, fiction — not to mention those books translated from the Chinese, French, and English. Reading, and the knowledge it brought, was good business. And now, for me, being well-read also turned out to be a good quality to have in acquiring a husband from such a learned village.

I found myself agreeing to go on supervised outings with Mr. Tai, walks around Hoan Kiem Lake or ice cream at a café. Even on those initial meetings, I noticed his taste for Western suits — always sharply creased, color coordinated, pocket kerchief at a precise angle. I also noted how he took special care to engage my chaperones — elder aunts and married cousins — in conversations. He sure charmed them. Not that I talked much to him at these meetings. Who would dare? We communicated mostly through the chaperones. I didn't even dare look into his eyes. I did steal glances at him once in a while, and the few times I caught him stealing glances at me — oh.

***

Was it "love"?

Such a strange word, a modern word. Once upon a time, unlike in fairy tales, nobody married for love. Rarely. People married for family, for security, for status, for business, for survival even. Love wasn't a right that my children would claim it to be when it was their turn to go off to build their families.

Maybe I was simply — finally — ready to marry at twenty-one, an old maid compared with my female relatives and friends. The wedding was in May 1939.

***

A sky of violet.

It was so pretty here right after sunset, the water on Hoan Kiem

Lake gently glistening, glowing in anticipation of the moon's nightly rendezvous.

"You're revisiting our history."

Don't look at him. Don't let him see you're glad to hear his voice instead of your own. The problem with talking to yourself is that after a while, you begin to doubt yourself.

Control your tone. "What are you doing here?" He glided over next to me on the red bridge. There was something different about him. Yes, he was now wearing a loose, plain black ao dai over white cotton pants. "You've changed."

He chuckled. "You can change anytime you want, too. Just focus on what you wish to wear, *et voilà.* It's one of the benefits of living in the netherworld."

"How did you find me? Why did you follow me?"

"You didn't want me to follow you?"

Sigh. You just can't talk to this man. Exactly like when he was alive. Ignore him. Just look at the water, how it's now as still as glass.

"Miss, listen. Do you remember the last time you were back in Ha Noi?"

"You return to Ha Noi all the time?"

"I was here with you in 1994, the first time you came back in four decades. You didn't feel my presence? I was there as you reunited with our cousins and returned to our old homes and businesses."

Madame Ty's mind shifted. When the United States ended the trade embargo on Viet Nam, I was already seventy-six, and those long, exhausting flights to return to my motherland nearly finished me. But I was determined. I wanted to come back as soon as travel was allowed between the two countries, no matter how much our cowardly children fretted about my health and the dangers of a communist regime. Well, this old woman was not scared. I knew those Viet Cong would see me for what I was, just an elderly exile who wanted to see her roots before she died. I wasn't coming back to try to start a revolution to overthrow communism. I was just someone with American dollars who could help anyone who wanted to help me. I figured the politics of the country might have changed, but the politics of money hadn't. And I was right.

"Agreed," Mr. Tai said, "you were fearless. Not like our cowardly children. You led and some of our offspring followed, then some of *their* offspring returned to Viet Nam, as well. Unseen, I accompanied them all. It always amazed me, observing them, like birds flying back to their nests or a river flowing back to its source, as the saying goes."

"Our cowardly children?"

He laughed. "Yes, unbelievably funny. They'd consult whatever addresses they remembered themselves or whatever you must have given them — the Savonta soap factory, my ancestral Hanh-Thien village home, our last villa in Ha Noi that we abandoned in 1954. Our descendants would give these addresses to the new taxi drivers or the cyclo pedalers. Then they'd always be surprised that the addresses still existed, the buildings still there, right down to the sign at the entrance to the soap factory that carried the names of our two oldest boys, Thai Loi — even though post-'54 squatters had long divided the property into houses and shops.

"I loved watching and listening to our descendants' reactions. What a pleasure to see Ha Noi through their eyes! It was like living our lives all over again."

But —

Mr. Tai looked at me. "Go ahead, ask."

"Did I say 'cowardly children' out loud or ..."

"Are you sure you're ready to talk about this?"

Just answer me.

"We seldom speak at all. I'm using my mouth to talk to you only because you're new."

We?

***

There is no, oh darling,
There is no first death

And there never will be
There never will be the last death
It's up to the self to know the self
And I know my own self

"Do you hear that?" Madame Ty asked out loud, then remembering what her husband just said, she thought her next question at him: Is it from a café overlooking the lake?

Before Mr. Tai could answer in any shape or form, Madame Ty, feeling awkward with this unfamiliar form of communication, started floating from one lit-up business to another. Not this café, she thought, not that much horn. And not there, I don't want to go near any electric guitar.

Mr. Tai followed her, speaking with his mouth. "Miss, I don't think what you think you're hearing is live music. I can see the words in your head. Is it a poem you once knew?"

"No," she answered distractedly, because she was suddenly drawn to a halo of what looked like twinkling fireflies in a corner of the lake. "This way."

Without looking back at her husband, she entered the halo. The light blinded her, but she could still hear the song's lyrics ahead, and she followed.

So tired, these legs of mine
Find the way to a bench to rest
So tired, this body of mine
Lie down with the earth forever
Look there are still so many people
Guiding one another 'round here

The light dimmed. And then it was very bright. Madame Ty blinked. A very bright room. A Buddhist monk in gold was chanting along with his assistants, somber in gray and brown robes, all facing rows and rows of people. I'm back in Arizona, she realized as she recognized the faces.

But it's a different day. The audience was now all dressed in black suits, even the women. And everyone was wearing white scarves on their foreheads! It's official then; it was a Vietnamese funeral. The thought chilled Madame Ty into standing very still, looking at all the ... mourners. An uneasy feeling spread from her head through her heart and into her feet. How will this end?

Turning, Madame Ty was relieved to see her husband beside her, back in his black French tux. "Can you believe it? Sir, look. They're not wearing the funeral white ao dai, but they do have the mourning headbands."

And the bands are even correct: plain white with tails for the fifteen grown children and their spouses; all the younger generations have no tails on their headscarves. On the front of the bands, just plain for the grandchildren, but a yellow dot for each great-grandchild, and a red dot for each great-great.

"It's impressive, don't you think, Sir, that this Americanized Vietnamese family of ours still respects the old traditions from the motherland?"

"Out of respect for you," Mr. Tai answered. "And they're setting a good example for the younger generations."

It must have been toward the end of the service because everyone was standing. Two lines of people inched toward the coffin from both sides of the hall, my children and their spouses first. Everyone was holding a blossom of some kind. Madame Ty watched as each person filing past placed a flower into the casket.

I don't remember doing this in Viet Nam.

She levitated until she was looking down at her physical body, which was almost covered with roses, chrysanthemums, daisies, and orchids. Then it struck her: Shouldn't I be crying? Why don't I feel anything for that corpse, the vessel that held me for nearly a century? Why am I not mourning for me?

Instead, she heard herself carelessly telling her husband, "I'm beginning to look like a garden."

No appreciative laughter. Not even a chuckle. Puzzled, Madame Ty came down to earth and found Mr. Tai intently watching the living shuffle past him.

Sensing his wife, he murmured, "Daughter, daughter, daughter. You didn't give me a son until my eighth child."

She shook her head. "And do you remember what you named your seventh daughter? Seven. Imagine how she felt. The older ones were Phoenix, Swallow, Virtue, Swan, Water, Peace. And then Seven."

"So, I gave up. Who knew? I should have saved a bird name for her, the one who turned out to actually have a singing voice. Anyway, Madame, let's not forget: It turned out all right. She renamed herself after she got older. Oanh. Oriole. She took care of herself. You don't think I was paying attention even in death? With all those American soldiers running around Sai Gon and our house full of girls, are you kidding? It's OK, as the Americans say. She married the most exotic spouse out of all our kids — a GI Joe of both Mexican and Native American blood."

"And what did you name the daughter who came after your first son? Nine!"

"I was depressed. I thought Thai was the only son I was going to get. Who knew the tenth child would also be a boy? But I felt better after that. I regained my hope there'd be more. Didn't I name the remaining girls properly? Madame, you can't blame me. Look at all of them. Count them. Fifteen and only four boys. Our last two children were truly sent by Heaven — both sons! I died happy."

You died happy! Here we are, looking like the day we got married and just started living together, and you died happy. Have you forgotten what happened?

"I knew you'd carry on just fine. Even back in Ha Noi, you were the real manager of our family businesses. I knew that. You always worked right through each pregnancy. And after each birth, you'd return to work in a week or so. Because it was your first love, the love of money. You were smart about how to make the money grow. I, on the other hand, loved my lifestyle. That's life, and we lost all of it. Blame war, blame politics, blame the times. I no longer care. Uncle! Do you remember Uncle? It broke my heart when he died. I didn't know how to start over in Sai Gon. But I knew you'd figure out a way. From the ice cream shop to ..."

"The house full of daughters." She interrupted. "No man around because our sons were too little. The two oldest daughters had their own families to take care of by then."

"I know, I know. In death, I saw all. And I was very proud of our younger daughters taking on manly responsibilities." Mr. Tai laughed. "I'll never forget seeing the disgust on the neighbors' faces when the girls climbed on top of the house to fix the roof because you couldn't afford to hire any man."

Despite her rage, giggles escaped Madame Ty before she could stifle them because she remembered the exact old-fashioned neighbors Mr. Tai was talking about. Oh, this husband of hers! He was so creative when he's trying to charm you, to unarm you.

It's up to the self to know the self
And I know my own self
One embraces all forms of life
Lying inside a woeful sound
Look there are still so many people
Guiding one another 'round here

Madame Ty stopped giggling. That wasn't a poem I once knew, she thought. Mr. Tai's face went blank. "Sir, even in death, am I still too quick for you?"

"Then what is it? Though it's starting to feel familiar to me, too. I can't get it out of my head."

Figuring that the new way to communicate was faster, Madame Ty said nothing as she concentrated on her memories of Khanh-Ly from the '70s: A young woman with a warm, low voice who married an anti-war songwriter, Trinh Cong Son.

Trinh Cong Son's music was very popular at our house during the war, she silently told Mr. Tai. Our children and their friends had to have music on all the time. They had to have the latest machines, recordings of the latest band. Not only Vietnamese, oh no. American. French. Spanish. British. A lot of guitars, gentle in Spanish, but the loud electric ones from America were deathly. R something R something. How strange, though, that it's Khanh-Ly I hear. I know she managed to come to America, too, but why would she come to my funeral?

Mr. Tai grinned at her. That was pretty good, Madame. Though as much as it will take for you to get used to giving images, it will take me that much to get used to receiving them from you.

Still chuckling over his wife's new power, he scanned the room. Well, Khanh-Ly is not here. She's in your head because someone in this room has her voice stuck in his head. I can hear her, too. We just have to find this person.

Madame Ty followed him down the line of bodies parading past her casket and then out among the pews. She was going around each person, but Mr. Tai just glided through everyone as if none of them existed in the mortal world, even taking shortcuts by passing right through the pews. "Wait, I can't keep up with you."

He glanced back. We're not here, Madame, remember? Walk right into them.

Even a man?

Don't worry; you won't feel a thing. Heaven knows I've tried.

You old goat. Even as a ghost you're a goat.

Oh, Madame, listen to you.

Actually, Madame Ty paused and looked around in wonder, listen to all these people around me. I can hear them! You don't understand. By the end, I was practically deaf, yet now I can hear conversations — even whispers!

"It's their grandmother's funeral. Why couldn't our children have dressed better?" "They don't live with us anymore. They're no longer little kids you can tell what to do all day."

"Why are we wearing these white bandages around our heads?" "It's a Vietnamese thing." "But it's like we're the walking wounded." "HA. You might have just hit on the true national identity."

"Oh, Inauguration Day was so cold! It had snowed and we were freezing. But I was determined to take HT and Thai-Binh. Thuan had to work at the paper, of course. We spent the night with friends on Capitol Hill so we could walk the next morning to the National Mall. It was really crowded, too, but everyone was so nice to each other. We were all happy to be there, be part of history, you know?"

"Mother didn't recognize anyone toward the end. We'd come visit and she'd ask for you. 'When's Duc coming home?' Duc this, Duc that. Otherwise, Mother didn't remember anybody's name." "Don't take it personally. I was her firstborn. That's the only reason she remembered my name."

"Oh yes, niece. Our last villa in Ha Noi is still standing. Some of our cousins still live there, so I checked on it when I was back. Though it's now surrounded by shops and cafes, you can still see the turret from the street, but of course, the villa itself is in terrible shape. When we lived there before 1954, your Ong Ngoai and Ba Ngoai rented out the bottom floor to a little school for girls. I was just a girl myself. When I saw that some of the students didn't have coats in the winter, I told your Ong Ngoai, and he not only bought jackets for those girls, he also paid for their education. I was so proud to have such a father."

"I can use some Starbucks." "Truong and I can do a run after this." "Well, remember to take the headscarves off." "Naah, Michaela can handle anyone who gives us trouble." "You mean just because your wife looks and sounds like Claudia Schiffer?"

"Your Ong Ngoai used to have a dog that he loved! The rest of us had to call him Uncle, and Uncle was fed steak and the best dishes that came out of the kitchen."

"Mom, you remember this dog Aunty is talking about?"

"My boy, your mother was too little. Aunt Phuong is the oldest; listen to her."

"Uncle slept on a silk bed."

"Now you're exaggerating."

"You don't believe me? What grade are you in?"

"I already have a job, Aunty."

"Oh, that's right! I forget who's who sometimes, too many nieces and nephews. Did you know I'm only ten years younger than Ba Ngoai? I was eleven when Ong Ngoai married her. But, Uncle, let me tell you, when the Japanese occupied Vietnam during World War II, I was seventeen. There was a famine under their occupation. People died right on the streets."

"Honestly?"

"It's true! We'd walk outside and there'd be bodies of whole families. Actually, just skin covering bones."

"Son, you have to know that your Ba Ngoai would always have the cook make a big pot of rice chicken soup and put it in front of our house so that people on the street could count on at least one bowl of food a day. Isn't that right, elder sister? First come, first served until the pot was emptied. Your grandmother was compassionate."

"Don't tell me the dog got put into the soup one day!"

"Nephew, are you kidding? Ong Ngoai *apologized* to Uncle for not being able to feed him steak anymore because of the famine. And he was crying when he was apologizing!"

***

What, what a thing to be remembered for. Madame Ty turned from the live conversation toward her husband. Did that stop you, too, Sir? Are you actually laughing? Maybe you're crying. It's all right, don't worry, I understand. Even a famine could be both tragedy and comedy. It had to be for those of us who survived. How could we live with ourselves otherwise? Sir, say something.

Continue our search. Without looking at his wife, Mr. Tai started flying through the living again.

Madame Ty followed. Sir, I forget, what are we looking for? But she didn't really wait for an answer because her ears were already tuning in to the nearest tête-a-tête.

"What are you reading?" "Somebody printed out the family tree. Look." "Sheesh, what year was Great-Grandma NOT pregnant?"

"She did not!" "Yes, she did. Dressed in her full traditional Vietnamese outfit, black teeth and all, she made a cyclo pedaler take her into the French Quarter and found the dancing hall. She marched straight in there, found Ong Ngoai locked in an embrace with a dancing girl, and pulled him by the EAR off that dance floor and back outside." "Wow." "She told him to get his ass home."

"What motherly love? She gave us life, then the maids took over. Besides the cook, the housekeeper, the gardener, and the driver, there were always several nursemaids around the house to constantly breastfeed babies. Your Ba Ngoai was a businesswoman, not a mother. I shall never forget one night. She was sleeping with a whole bunch of us, and somehow my head ended up near her bottom. She was menstruating, and I was woken up by this heavy smell and this thick liquid on my head. I screamed. I thought my head was bleeding and I was dying. A maid came and got me and cleaned me up. I wasn't of age yet to get monthlies. The maid had to explain to me how blood got on my head. And your Ba Ngoai, she hardly showed concern that she had bled on me. She was just annoyed she had soiled herself and had to get up in the middle of the night to go get cleaned up. To this day, if I don't wash my hair soon enough, I can still smell that metallic odor on my head!"

**

Madame Ty froze in shock. Sensing Mr. Tai nearby, she raised her hands. Don't touch me.

He sighed. She was just upset you're gone.

Sir, don't touch me. It was how I got pregnant year after year. Did you think I wanted that many children? Fifteen didn't even count the twins who had died.

You're forgetting now. You're forgetting the context. It was a different time.

Do you think I liked having my body out of commission nine months out of the year, year after year? Thank Heaven our granddaughters don't have to go through what I did.

You never minded me touching you.

Who wants to talk about that with you?

Then let's talk about them.

She looked around the filled room. I don't care. They can't all be ours.

Mr. Tai chuckled. Well, yes, many friends of the family have come to pay their respect to you. It was only natural. Our children were among the first Vietnamese refugees to resettle in this state of Arizona in '75, so they knew a lot of people, and a lot of people knew you. Nevertheless, all those with the headbands are ours. Miss, I knew you'd appreciate this, so I did the math. See here: Of our one hundred and forty children, grandchildren, and so forth, ninety or so are here for you.

Truly?

Count for yourself: All fifteen of our children and ten of their spouses are here. Forty-six of our grandchildren and spouses. Nineteen great-grandchildren and even a couple of great-great-grandchildren.

Madame Ty looked around and finally saw the two with red dots on their white headbands.

Yes, you found the sister and brother. Look at those pudgy cheeks and all that brown, curly hair. The curls are from their Egyptian mother.

Our bloodline now includes Egyptian? I don't remember going to this wedding. Did they fly me to ...?

That's not all. We have a pregnant great-granddaughter married to a Taiwanese; they're due next month so that's why she couldn't fly to Arizona. And a granddaughter here in the room is also pregnant — that's her in line with the American husband with the beard. They're due next year.

No African American blood yet? But we just got our first black president.

Heaven and earth, woman, you're hilarious! You're so competitive that being an ancestor to doctors, lawyers, engineers, and bankers isn't good enough? What's this! Look at you holding my hand. Don't, Miss. Don't pull away. I like holding your hand. I like to see you so happy. He laughed. Yes, I know. You're just happy with the numbers. For you, looking at all our descendants is like looking at money in the bank, isn't it? Agreed, you and I will live forever through them.

***

A man spoke into the microphone: "As soon as you're done paying your respects, please go outside to enjoy the home cooking the family has laid out on the tables. Only the children of the deceased and their spouses can follow the priest to the cremation room."

I asked for cremation?

I mean, yes, go right ahead and follow my wishes — as long as I'm not going to feel the flames. Right, Mr. Tai? Where ... That man, gone again. Typical, disappearing when I most need him. Though why I should suddenly feel so attached to that body in there was beyond me. Who cared? It wasn't as if blood flowed through it, not as if it had a future.

Everyone was following the man's instructions except several little ones. By the yellow dots on their headbands, these were some of my great-grandchildren, so I assumed they didn't understand Vietnamese.

Look at my children — so wrapped up in their grief that nobody realized these three little kids weren't supposed to be anywhere near the cremation room. I hadn't plan on seeing what happened to my body, but I couldn't just abandon my great-grandkids.

What a life: Even in death I must manage things.

Up ahead, my sons and sons-in-law were carrying the casket across the threshold. Out here in the hallway, my daughters and daughters-in-law were crying so much, you'd think they were the ones at death's door. Maybe I shouldn't be here after all. Too many people in this narrow space.

Calm down. Vu Thi Ty, stay. What are you afraid of? Look at you. If you were still breathing, you'd be holding your breath. Such weakness. Be practical. After all, you're free of that body. You're out here and you're invisible. You no longer could feel a thing.

The men have returned to the hallway, all except my youngest one, the son my husband named Thuong, meaning reward — because he had been born about the time Mr. Tai had realized his own days were numbered. My youngest was still in that chamber and, oh, he pushed that button. There I go ... sliding out of the casket along with all those pretty blossoms everyone had laid on me. The scent of those flowers! And there was that other ... a very faint, just a hint, of heat. Breathe. Breathe. Don't faint. Let me ignore these mortals, just let me squeeze in among their bodies to lean against the wall. Feel that wall. Feel your body leaning against the wall. Still here. Thank Heaven I was right! I didn't feel a thing. Blessed Buddha.

Just think, in that big oven, the blue and golden fire was dancing and feasting on flowers, silk brocade, flesh, and bone. Out here? Out here, I was beyond its reach. Yes, Vu Thi Ty, now you can laugh. No one can hear you. Now you can really say that body had nothing to do with you anymore. If you knew how to dance, you'd dance, too, along with the flames.

Who was making all that noise? Ah, the three great-grandchildren were whimpering and crying at seeing more than they had bargained for. Finally, now their elders noticed them! Yes, Duc, get them out of here.

Had this hallway always been this narrow? Too many faces, too many bodies, too much chanting and wailing. Mr. Tai, where are you? Come out from wherever you are and get me out of here. Ughh, I'll have to pass through both the women and the men.

Is that you, Sir, in the back of this broken-down crowd?

That husband of mine, puffing on one of those thin cigars as if he were at a party. Who were those people with him, fading in and out of the shadows? They weren't crying at all, not even a frown. Their faces were blank, even peaceful. Why were they at my funeral?

***

I'm flying. ... But I can't see! I can't see and all I hear is the roar of the wind. Mr. Tai, where are you? Oh Mr. Tai, it's dark and it's freezing, the wind like a burn on my face. Where are you?

Where am I going? I beg you Heaven and Buddha, please rescue me from this thin air. I want to land. Yes, just like this. Oh, thank Your Holiness, thank You for listening to my prayers. Thank You, Your Holiness, for stopping the whirlwind.

What's under me?

Steady your feet. Don't panic. Compose yourself. If a heavenly court suddenly appeared, be ready to defend your life. You have done much good. You have donated to so many charities. You have helped so many people. You had all those children, yet you still adopted many young people. They'd tell their stories of need and you'd feel for them and take care of them, too.

Whoever the deity about to make his entrance to judge over my soul must already know that. I have to believe that Your Holiness already knows that. And You must also have seen that in my old age, I became more tolerant and sympathetic to the changing times. Live and let live, one of my grandchildren used to tell me, and it was true. I had started to argue but then realized I couldn't disagree, not with the new norm of living in America. Live and let live was the new once upon a time.

It's so cold and dark. Please Heaven and Buddha, have mercy on me. Where am I?

Why can't I hear anything? Nothing. It's too hushed. Except the wind. But what a lonely sounding wind. Nothing stirring in it.

You can't stay here forever, Madame Ty nagged herself. Do something.

But that husband, he was just here. Where is he?

Thinking of Mr. Tai abandoning her again made Madame Ty feel sorry for herself, a feeling she detested. Which made her angry and impatient with herself.

Pathetic old woman! Why are you counting on that man to show you the way when, after his passing, you lived nearly five decades just fine without him?

Think about it: Your earthly ties with this man defined you as a woman, though you knew him for only twenty-three out of the ninety years of your life. Not even a full quarter-century! You were alone before you were born, and now that you're done with that life, you're alone again.

Again, and now what? What was I supposed to do, just wait here? For how long? So cold.

Please, Higher Being, whoever Your Holiness might be, if You're there, then You already know me. You've seen the high and low points of my mortal existence. You already know my life was not of evil deeds. It was full of hard work. Work was all I knew.

It was the only reason why I was difficult to live with when I came to America. I confess. That was my sin against my children. But they didn't understand. All they wanted for me was to rest, insisting I take it easy in my old age.

And what did they know of old age? They were using the Vietnamese norm. So was I. I, too, thought I was ready to relax, to prepare my body for its descent into death. What a laugh.

I was not even sixty, not even of retirement age in America. From running a mini empire in Ha Noi to a business or two in Sai Gon to running nothing — not even my own household. What did I do with myself all day in the Valley of the Sun? TV. Grandchildren. Watering the garden. Being driven to temple. Buddhist services. Vietnamese community festivals. All well and good. But there was also just the endless day after day, month after month of plain breathing in and out and not knowing what to do with myself. From above, Your Holiness must have seen and pitied me.

It weren't as if I could walk outside in that Arizona neighborhood of spotless sidewalks and vanilla-color house after vanilla-color house and pass the time away talking to my neighbors. Everybody was at work or in school. And even if anyone were home during the day, I couldn't speak any of the languages — American, Mexican, or Native American.

Not like in Viet Nam, where extended families lived mixed in with the shops and there had always been conversations, traffic, food vendors. Life. Was it any wonder I passed the time making mischief among my children?

I confess, Your Holiness, it was true. I'd call one son and badmouth his brother. Or I'd tell a daughter that the other siblings had been bad-mouthing her. I admit it. I was bored. But should I be punished for that?

Once, a granddaughter, the firstborn of my firstborn, asked whether I'd prefer to live out the rest of my days in Viet Nam. Thuan, in fact, had moved back to live in Sai Gon a couple of years with her American husband, so she knew we still had plenty of cousins near and far who'd take care of me there, not to mention what remained of my numerous unofficial adopted children.

I was tempted. I won't deny it.

Of course, even if I decided to, my children wouldn't have allowed it. You see, they'd never forgive themselves if anything happened to me in Viet Nam and they were too far away to do anything.

And, honestly, I guess I felt too guilty to be so selfish. What kind of woman would I have been if I didn't want to be near my children and grandchildren? They were — every single one of them — in America after all. Every year, like clockwork, there was a wedding of some grandchild or another. Every year, another soul would be born into the family, some years two or three, adding to the lifespan of the Nguyen clan. I had worked so hard to build a nest and a family, and now it was reproducing itself without me having to do anything at all.

Another way to look at it, the clan was like a bank account with annual interest, growing and growing while I sat back and watched. I didn't want to miss a minute.

This can't be. This can't be my hell. Please, Buddha, no, to be stuck here in the dark all alone forever, talking to myself to the end of time. Don't cry. How dare you! Consider the alternatives. Hush.

Enough. Take a step. Walk! Not as easy as I hoped. I can't see what it is but my velvet slippers, the ground, it's soft, and my slippers are getting wet.

I thought this was to be the Golden Springs of the ancient texts. Or the Nine Springs. Of course, we all knew it was just a literary, poetic way of talking about the netherworld. Even so, don't tell me that I was the only mortal to have imagined the Nine Springs as a lush, tropical paradise, with waterfalls, and dances by elegant angels. Not the golden-hair ones dressed in white ball gowns from those Christmas mangers I used to see at churches during Christmas. More like those from Chinese paintings, with jeweled pins holding up their elaborately constructed hair and long, silk sleeves swirling around their hand-embroidered chiffon robes of every color in the rainbow.

I thought I'd see souls playing chess while drinking rice wine and eating all sorts of exotic meats and fruits. I thought there'd be poetry contests, art classes, the option to go to the theater to watch your descendants — there way below the clouds — play out their lives.

This is certainly not the tropics. I don't hear any waterfall. No, don't try to guess what you're walking through. I would gladly hand over all this cold jewelry on me right now if I knew what — NO, don't think of what, whether it has teeth or ...

You listen, Madame Ty. Lift your leg above whatever, of course it's the ground. Lift the other leg, move forward. That's it.

Wait, wait. How could I forget? I'm no longer mortal; I must glide. Why am I trying to walk through whatever it is!? Which would you rather have, fire or ice?

Oh Heaven. Is that what this is? Snow? Heaven and earth. I never saw any in Viet Nam, but my children took me several times to see snow in the Arizona mountains.

Thank Heaven. Heaven and Buddha, please let it be. Yes, this feels like powdered ice falling between my fingers. I bet my past life that's what I'm moving through. I never imagined I'd be so happy to be walking in snow!

Do I hear the tinkling of a bell?

"Madame, can you hear me? Follow my voice."

"Mr. Tai! Is that you? Where have you been? One minute I was talking to you, the next minute you were gone, and it was very dark!"

"I've been waiting for you."

"Waiting for me? But where are we?" There was that faint tinkling again.

"Yes, go toward the little wind chime. I'm standing right underneath it. Here, I'll light a match for you to follow."

A yellow flicker appeared and grew brighter. Now that I remembered to glide, I met the little light in no time, and behind the match, I saw my husband's smile. "Sir, are you taunting me? Why didn't you do this sooner?"

"Madame, I can't tell by your face whether you're angry or scared, but stop looking at me like that. How can I let you inside looking like that?"

"Inside where? What if I don't want to go inside?"

Mr. Tai just turned and passed through a white door. Of course. Never mind how I feel, never mind what I want. I want to get out of these wet clothes.

"Madame," his body reappeared, "take my hand and come in out of that snow."

What did you say?

"Yes. Here, I'll show you."

Where did all that moonlight come from? Ah! It really *is* snow, everywhere, on the yard, the bushes, the cars.

Mr. Tai shook his head. "Isn't it beautiful? The very first time I saw snow was in the afterlife, and I was like a kid with a new toy."

But look at this huge, old tree. "How can it be winter when there are fat, white blossoms on the branches?"

"This tree I had never seen until here in the American South. A magnolia, which usually, yes, blooms white flowers as big as plates. But those aren't flowers. It's all clumps of snow on the dark leaves. I still haven't figured out how magnolias don't lose their leaves in autumn like other trees."

"The American South?"

"Well, it's really Northern Virginia, just outside Washington, D.C. They keep moving the line on where the South is." He winked at me.

I hit his arm. I couldn't help it. "That wasn't what I meant, and you knew it. You knew how nervous I was back at the funeral. And just now I was freezing in the dark out here for so long, not knowing where I was going. I don't care where we are as long as it's no hell of fire. Do you promise? Say it."

"Madame," he said, grinning, "have you forgotten? Buddhism says your soul is not decided until the hundredth day after your passing."

She covered her eyes. "Oh Heaven, Heaven I forgot." She uncovered her eyes. "I was so terrified that I forgot."

"Well, that's what Buddhism says."

"Why must you be so cruel? True or not?"

"Why don't you walk through this door?"

Why don't you tell me what's on the other side?

***

"Madame," Mr. Tai said as he melted into the house, "use your nose."

Distracted by her husband's odd command, she followed him and, as her eyes adjusted, found herself in an entryway.

She turned and saw that the white door was now behind her. Next to it, as if on sentry, hung a life-size, black-and-white drawing of a British knight in full armor, his black sword sheathed and hanging from his waist. Nervously, she looked up into his face. His eyes stared back down at her, but no, they were not alive. The only message coming from the knight was in his hands, straight fingers and palms pressed together. Feeling brave, Madame Ty asked, "If you're praying, why isn't your head bowed?"

Nothing stirred from beneath the glass covering the print. But out of the corner of her eye, she caught strands of wispy smoke that her nose identified as the fragrance of incense. She turned toward the drifting smoke and saw an open cabinet, its glass side panels decorated with swirling, carved wood. On the cabinet's roof, silk flowers wove among statues of the most revered of all the Buddhas — the prince who formed the religion in India before the era of Jesus Christ, his thin body sitting in lotus position. There was the Buddha of Compassion, vertically regal in her full robe; and the earth deity, sprawling out fat and bald and beaming a thick-lipped grin, the one most non-Asians confused to be the original Buddha.

On two deep shelves below the Buddhas were framed photographs,

RENDEZVOUS AT THE ALTAR - 159

mostly black and white, surrounding a bowl of lit incense, flickering candles, a miniature tea set carved from stones and another from porcelain, and fresh flowers.

A family altar, she realized, but whose?

Madame Ty drifted closer to peer into the photographs. Several of the black-and-white ones were of someone's ancestors dressed in dark turbans and ao dais. Not only were their clothes old-fashioned, so were the ways they were staged — immobile from the shoulders up, staring straight into the camera; sitting erect, staring down at an ancient book; standing erect with one hand at the hip and the other holding a fan; standing erect, staring straight into the camera and one hand holding a branch of some potted, flowering tree.

From the dark, uneven ink, Madame Ty recognized that these photographs were taken during the French colonial days. Back then, only the very rich Vietnamese had the means to have their portraits taken, by professionals who came with bulky, messy equipment — unlike the modern times Madame Ty just departed, in which cameras were so cheap that children got them as Christmas presents, in which technology had shrunk the cameras and put them into handheld phones.

What changes I have witnessed in nearly a century! Madame Ty congratulated herself. She leaned toward the old pictures as if she could step inside those frames and those colorless, faraway days.

AH! "Mr. Tai, your mother and father," she exclaimed and simultaneously glided backward because the pair suddenly floated out of their frames and descended right in front of her.

"Miss Ty, we've been eagerly awaiting your arrival."

She didn't know how but she managed to keep her wits about her, answering and bowing at the same time out of an old habit she thought had died long ago with her elders. "I beg your pardon, Father, Mother, I was too slow in finding my way."

"Miss Ty," her mother-in-law said, "no need to kowtow to us."

Obediently, she straightened up, quickly touching her head wrap to make sure no lock of hair had escaped. Surreptitiously, she started smoothing out her ao dai just in case it had wrinkled and was relieved to find that the long tunic somehow changed from her velvet wedding gown to a thick, dark brocade. Ty stood straight but still kept her eyes respectfully down. "I beg your pardon, Mother and Father, if I had forgotten anything, if I had come unprepared. It was ... such a long day. And I didn't know where I was going."

"You were following our son," her father-in-law said, using his fan to point back to the altar. There was Mr. Tai in a frame, all rigid in a cream suit. But his mouth quickly curved into a smirk as he left the altar to return to Ty's side.

He didn't float out alone. With him was one of the other women in traditional clothes. "You two never met in life. This is Nguyen Thi Gai, my first wife."

The elder wife smiled, her glossy, black-stained teeth proudly reflecting her time. "Finally, I have the honor to meet you, Miss Ty. Pardon me. I should call you Madame Tai. You were married to our husband longer than I was."

Ty was so preoccupied with wondering whether her own teeth were black again, just like Gai's, that it took her a minute to answer. "Oh no, Madame, you were the first. I hope you found that I did not fail in my duties toward our husband and your daughters."

"From the spirit world, I observed you all those years and grew grateful to you." Nguyen Thi Gai bowed. "I learned about you, too, from your son-in-law," she said, lifting an arm back to the altar.

Out of which emerged a clean-shaven South Vietnamese military officer wearing black-frame glasses. Madame Ty was astonished and shaken when she recognized him as Nghia, the husband of her firstborn.

"Mother, it's a privilege to welcome you to our home. Mother, please Mother, do not cry."

Madame Ty wiped her eyes but couldn't stop the sobs escaping her throat. "Look at how pathetic I am. I didn't shed a tear at my own funeral and now ... but yours was the first death that struck our clan in America." She pointed at his face as tears streamed down hers. "You were only fifty-eight. You weren't supposed to depart life before I did.

At last, I joined you, two decades later! It just proves that fate is not fair at all."

Nghia took her hand and touched her shoulder. "I'm all right, Mother. I'm at peace."

Madame Ty, remembering they were not alone, straightened herself and lifted a sleeve to dab her eyes. "I'm all right now. Elder brother Nghia, you said this is your home?"

He smiled. "I visit all my children and grandchildren in their different homes, but Duc lives here, Mother. This is my base camp to be near my wife."

"She must have moved here after I was too weak to fly on an airplane. I don't recognize this house at all."

"Duc has set up this altar for all of us," Nghia said. "My side of the family's here, too, waiting to welcome you. First is someone you never met in life, someone whom I followed around as a little boy — my Ong Noi, Mr. Nguyen Xuan Trach."

On the altar, the old scholar lifted his kind eyes from the book he was reading and rose out onto the carpeted floor. He wore a rigid, black turban as if it were a top hat and, over his white pants, his black cotton ao dai was as crisp as if it had just been steamed and pressed.

"Sir." The newcomer bowed from her waist.

"Miss Ty, I've heard so much about you from my favorite grandson. Nghia goes on and on about what a kind mother-in-law you were to him. For that, I'm in your debt. I look forward to sharing with you what this," he waved at his surroundings, "is all about. I've been in this nether-world since 1949, so I have a few theories. But that's for later. There's plenty of time for that later."

"Mother," Nghia said, "you remember my father? Le Tat Tien."

"Of course. Greetings, Sir." Madame Ty bowed and noticed that he was also dressed in a cream suit, just like her husband.

"Madame Ty, I hope your long journey here was not too tiring. I'm usually in Viet Nam because most of my children and grandchildren are still there. But the wives and I attended your funeral and came straight here in order to welcome you."

"You were there? But why didn't you say anything?"

Nghia's father smiled. "We didn't want to overwhelm you at your memorial service. It was decided we'd wait until you found your way here."

On either side of him were two women, both in the same dark traditional clothing, yet they couldn't look any more different — one had a face all angles and panes, the other was a full moon. The first nodded her head. "Madame, do you remember who I am?"

Ty looked into the sharp eyes over the high cheekbones and recognized Nghia's stepmother. "Madame Kim, you look a lot younger than when I saw you last."

"As do you. You'll see that we get to choose what age to be now. Well, most of the time." She stepped aside. "Madame Ty, allow me to introduce you, then, to my predecessor. This is elder sister Nguyen Thi Nhuan." And the other traditionally dressed woman nodded, her round face even younger than that of her husband's second wife.

"Yes, Madame Ty. In life I did always look younger than my age, something I passed onto my descendants, and then I had the misfortune of dying young, on a boat back to my village. I was only forty-two."

Madame Ty grasped her hands. "Elder sister, I remember now. You had four sons."

Nghia, standing beside his mother, said, "Reuniting with her in this world was a tremendous blessing for me. She helped me find peace. She even likes to tease that I was sixteen years older than her when I departed life."

The moon-face woman laughed with ebony teeth and touched her son's shoulder. "Nghia, we have others to introduce to your mother-in-law."

Nghia took Madame Ty by the arm and led her deeper into the room. "Mother, this is a rather unconventional ancestral altar, as you might have noticed. There are Americans here with us."

A Hollywood-looking woman clasped Ty's hands. With her fair skin, rouged mouth, wavy hair that ended at the ears, and a black dress that ended just below the knees, she looked as if she had just stepped off a black-and-white movie screen.

"Awww," exclaimed the woman with the light-colored eyes. "You're so kind, Madame Ty, to think of me that way. I'm so relieved you made it through, and that you and Tai can be together again."

"Forgive my wife, Madame," said a square-face gentleman in a dark suit. "Let us introduce ourselves. This is Anne, and I am Carroll. Our youngest daughter, Carol Anne, lives here with her husband, Bob Sr., and your daughter Duc. Can you believe it? We still can't, though they've been living this way since 2001."

Ty couldn't take her eyes off their mouths, trying to absorb that this American couple was speaking directly to her, with no translators. Three decades of her refugee life dragged by because she couldn't communicate, frustrated that she was made mute by not knowing the American tongue, and here the words and their meanings and images were just washing over her. She understood all and saw all. She was so excited and so full of questions that she was having a hard time moving her mind, let alone her tongue.

The turbaned old scholar, son-in-law Nghia's grandfather, peered at the newly born spirit. "Of course, you must understand, Miss Ty, language for us now is no longer really language. Your mind is dead, but your soul is alive."

"Sir?"

"Don't worry, Miss Ty, your soul will come to accept that your mind is no longer there, and you'll leave behind old habits, such as understanding everything only in Vietnamese terms. Do you remember what one of your descendants called you at your wake — a drug runner?" He chuckled.

"Yes, yes, but I didn't understand it, Sir."

"What your old habit of a mind remembers is that the term does not exist in Vietnamese. She was speaking in English. What your soul received was an image of what she was thinking of when she spoke. It's not the same at all. But your old habit was to try to translate the image, as if it were language, into Vietnamese."

"Miss," her husband said, "that's how we're all communicating in this room."

Images. The scholar nodded at her, his lips immobile. Not words.

Carroll chuckled. "Though I have to tell you, Madame, even images can get lost in translation between the Americans and the Vietnamese in our family. It turns out, different cultures can even have different images for what we mean, for our opinions, in how we judge things. But for those of us who have been together on this altar, we have come to know each other very well."

Even images can be misunderstood? Ty touched her temple, afraid she's too frozen to ever express herself again.

Don't worry, a collective thought rose. We can read your mind.

Which, instead of making her feel better, irked Ty and jolted her into speaking. "But how do you like being forced to exist together with our family on this altar?" she managed to ask the foreign couple. "You never thought you would be on one, am I right? You're not Buddhist, and Americans certainly don't worship ancestors like we Vietnamese do."

"Well, who wouldn't want to be worshiped?" Anne giggled.

"Madame Ty, you're absolutely right," Carroll said. "And no, we're Christians. But it has been a pleasure, an absolute pleasure mixing it up with your family. In life, we loved our trips to the Orient! But I had never imagined how immersed we'd be in Asian culture in our afterlife. Never in a million years would I have bet on it! Isn't afterlife funny?" He grinned and waited, but when he got no response from the newcomer, he lowered his eyes and cleared his throat. "Yes, how did we get here?" He looked at his wife.

"When Big Bob and Carol Anne moved in with Bob and Thuan, and her mother," Anne said. "That's when our daughter asked them whether we could join the altar club. See?" She glanced at the altar, and Ty finally noticed a gold-framed photo of older versions of Carroll and Anne in sportswear, as if they had just finished a round of golf.

Carroll put his arms around his wife. "The point is, we couldn't be more grateful to be accepted into this club. Let me tell you, Madame, we've been members of quite a few country clubs. This one's not only a lot of fun, but we're also learning so much. Tai takes us on trips whenever he visits all your other children, to Viet Nam even. He's our personal tour guide and history teacher."

"It doesn't hurt that the bar's just around the corner!" Anne laughed. And so did Mr. Tai. Ty eyed him while Carroll frowned at Anne.

Mr. Tai looked from Anne to his wife. "Miss, no, really. The ancestral altar literally is around this corner from the family bar. Come look if you don't believe me."

It was only then that Ty sensed the space around her. She had been so busy meeting or reacquainting herself with one spirit after another that she hadn't had time to see where she was. Beneath her beaded slippers was beige carpeting. The walls were covered in a print of little birds, butterflies, and delicate branches supporting fragile flowers — everything in such a balance of green, gold, brown, and red that the print could bring forth spring as well as autumn.

Where Ty was standing, the altar was on the left. Opposite the altar, a huge mirror framed in black and gold hung over a black low cabinet, painted with orange and gold flowers, birds, and dancers from India. On her right, in front of a bay window, a telescope stood between two dark green velvet chairs. Nearby hung a gold-framed, small print of one of those French paintings of ballerinas.

On the wall in front of Ty, there was a giant vertical oil painting of a Vietnamese New Year market scene: red paper lanterns hovering as if they were UFOs, ceramic buckets of orange kumquats nestling in dark green leaves, women with sidelong glances dressed in colorful ao dais, men with their mouths shaped like O's. The Tet painting hung over an ornately curved sofa of dark brown teak. On the sofa were pillows in silk and velvet that picked up the colors from the wallpaper and the oil painting.

To the left of the sofa, there was a dark brown dining set in front of another bay window. But you couldn't eat there; the table beneath the chandelier was set with two computers and a printer.

To the left of the bay window hung a wooden panel that took up the width of the wall. The panel was carved with faceless people beneath birdcages, some containing birds and some empty. Madame Ty suddenly found herself in front of the carved art. The people, she saw, had heads of blank circles big and small with bodies of long triangles or vertical rectangles. The panel was mostly beige and military green, with bursts of gold here and there. Like on that lone bird free of the cages, or on that lone cage holding a faceless couple.

From those birdcages, Ty turned left again, looking for her husband. But she saw, just around the corner from the altar, as promised, the bar. On a wheeled, winged piece of furniture were bottles and glasses of varying sizes. Above the bar hung two square lacquer paintings: In the yellow one, a maiden wearing a virginal white ao dai, the ubiquitous Vietnamese high school uniform for girls, held a conical straw hat under a flame tree to catch its scarlet blossoms. In the red one, a nude knelt over a vase of lotus blooms already beginning to wilt, the white petals and green stalks vivid against the river of black hair flowing from her tilted head into the bottom of the frame.

The lacquer paintings' dominant colors and the stark contrasts of the two female subjects so captivated Ty, she didn't notice someone was at her side. "Madame Ty?" Turning, she saw a white-haired woman wearing glasses smiling hesitantly at her.

"Welcome, Madame Ty. I'm Mary. I'm new here, too. I came to this altar in 2004. My grandson married your granddaughter."

Something about this gentle old woman made Ty grasp both her hands. As she did, images of a bride in a pink hand-painted silk ao dai and a groom in a white dinner jacket flooded her mind. Ty chuckled. "We met at their wedding in Southern California, am I correct?"

Mary looked at Mr. Tai's first wife. "Madame Gai, you were right. She does have shiny black teeth just like yours!" Seeing Ty's hands rushing to cover her mouth, Mary's hands flew up to hers. "Oh, I'm so sorry. I wasn't laughing at your teeth. I was just telling them I don't remember you having black teeth at the wedding. That's all."

Ty glided to the mirror and tentatively smiled at her younger self.

They sure were! "But, oh," she turned to ask the others excitedly, "does this mean I get to chew betel nuts again?"

Gai grinned. "We'll all have to travel back to northern Viet Nam together."

Those in Western clothing were hanging out by the bar, pouring Courvoisier into their tumblers. All except Mary. "Madame Mary," Ty asked, looking around, "is your husband here?"

Mary blushed. "Are you talking about Hal? My ex-husband's still alive. Out of the four sets of grandparents for Bob and Thuan, Hal's the only one left standing."

Mr. Tai raised his glass. "To Hal's health."

"Yes, Hal Elston's outliving us all," Carroll said of his daughter's father-in-law. "Maybe he'll last to a hundred. What do you think, Mary? Which picture of Hal will the grandkids pick for the altar when he finally makes it here? The black-and-white one of him all pecs and a six-pack instead of abs, wearing those 1930s swim shorts complete with a belt? That would drive all the ladies on the altar crazy. Right, Anne? Or maybe a color photo of him playing softball way into his seventies."

"I look forward to meeting this Hal," said Tien, the former postmaster, as he lifted his cognac. *"Mon Dieu!"*

"Ah, non," Tai said, touching his glass to Tien's. "As the kids now say: OMG."

Mary looked down. "I worry about Hal, actually."

Ty threw the three grandfathers a sharp glance before guiding Mary to sit with her on the sofa underneath the Tet painting. "Why?"

"When you met us, I was with my second husband, John. And Hal had Vi."

"Oh! Vi. That's his lady friend. I remember them dancing!"

"Yes, well, he's still taking her dancing every Friday, but she's no longer living with him."

"She was living with him?"

The white-haired woman dressed in senior-citizen American casual wear looked into the eyes of the raven-haired woman dressed in formal Vietnamese clothes, and grinned. "Just listen to me. I'm really talking to you. Not like at the wedding, when all we could do was smile at each other across all that food." Mary shook her head. "I'm sorry, I'm not explaining myself very well. I keep thinking that you and I have known each other for years, and that you already know a lot of this stuff because, you know, through our mutual family I've gotten to know a lot about you. Isn't that funny? And then, too, there's the fact that I just attended your funeral, and I heard so much there. I keep forgetting we met only once in real life."

"It's all right." Ty patted Mary's hand, as if they had been dead together forever. "I'm listening."

"I'll start over. Vi had been living with Hal as if they were husband and wife for decades. Just not on paper. She had been divorced, too, so they just didn't want to get married again."

"How sensible."

"Do old Vietnamese people do that? Just live together ... well, I don't want to say in sin."

Ty smirked. "You'd be surprised. But Hal and Vi."

"I'm sorry, I get distracted. Vi has been getting weaker and weaker, and her daughters had to move her into a nursing home, something similar to where I lived out my last days. It was close enough that Hal could still visit her, and she would come spend weekends with him and, you know, go dancing every Friday night. But she's been faking it, and he doesn't know it."

"Faking it?"

"Oh, I feel so guilty even talking about all this popping in and out. Not like the others here on the altar; they love zooming around the world, visiting live people. We spirits really can be like the fly on the wall, you know, see everything and hear everything but people don't see us. It's fun, I'll admit, and it's reassuring on some levels. Still, I always feel guilty doing it. But I can't help it. I want to see that my survivors are OK. So, I pop in on Hal, on our kids, on the grandkids now all grown with their own kids."

"What's Vi faking?"

Mary took a deep breath. "Consciousness. Her mind would go blank, and when it came back, she'd have to pretend she had heard, and seen, everything and had been present. Whether it's at a dance, watching TV, or whatever. It's awful. I feel so bad for them. She and Hal have been such a great couple. Now Vi's slipping away, and Hal realizes it, but he doesn't accept how bad it really is. When I visit them in Colorado, I could barely watch them. I mean, when you get down to it, she's abandoning him, and he doesn't accept it yet. And she's not the only one."

"There have been other women?"

"I mean Hal's friends, old colleagues from decades ago, or men he played softball with all these years. They're all dying off, or they've become too sick. I mean, none of us took care of our bodies like Hal does. He even prefers his vegetables raw, to capture all the nutrients, you know? He's always done everything possible to take care of his body, but not because it's good. I'll tell you the real reason: Hal has been obsessed with exercising his whole life and watching what he eats because he's scared of death. He is. He and our son Bob, they're on a mission to cheat death. If they had it their way, they'd live forever."

Ty chuckled. "I'm sure they know they can't live forever."

Mary shook her head. "I guess I'm not ... I haven't hit the nail on the head. They're on a mission to live as long as they can, and cheat old-age diseases."

"Ah! Then it seems Mr. Hal has succeeded. He's outlasting even his younger companion."

"But that's just it, Madame Ty. This is where I start worrying about him. His peers have been dying off, and now his woman's going, or what's left of her mind. What's the use of taking care of your body and cheating old age if everyone who means anything to you passes away before you do? I mean, it's true that Hal wins. He's the last one standing. But now what? Is a painless old age really worth the loneliness of your last days? No spouse, no friends, the kids and grandkids live far away. It's just you, what's left of your mind, and your caregivers. Is that living? Is that living worth all those tricks, the exercising, and avoiding fats and sugar? And what's the use of a healthy body if you don't have a healthy mind to go with it?"

Ty stared blankly at Mary. "I never exercised in my life."

Mary furrowed her brows. "Hal's so lonely, that's all I'm saying. Even while sitting with Vi, he's so lonely. Because she's just not the same chatty Vi. On her weekend visits, he's like her caregiver, you know? It's like a long goodbye. He knows she's not the same, and he's afraid of what's coming. He just doesn't know when. Oh, Ty, you won't believe how painful it is for me to visit them these days."

"But they're both still alive," Ty insisted.

"Are they?" Mary asked, looking around the room. "We've been debating that."

"What do you mean?" Ty asked out of habit, but her mind's already receiving images and voices from the prior discussions on the family altar. "Oh."

Mary's eyes found the ancient, Vietnamese scholar, sitting at the dining table and staring at one of the computer screens. "Sir," the American woman said, "won't you please come help me?"

The old gentleman turned and, intuitively, Ty realized he had been anticipating the plea. "Miss Mary, I hesitate to interrupt your talk with Miss Ty."

Mary answered, "But you've been doing the most research on this."

Ty looked from the woman who died in the American Midwest just five years ago to the man who passed away in northern Vietnam six decades ago, and she sensed a teacher-student respect. In awe of the unearthly relationship, Ty rose. "Sir, please take my seat."

"Miss, please stay." The old scholar chose one of the green side chairs. "Miss Ty, what you're seeing and hearing in your head, is it clear enough?"

"No, Sir. It's all jumbled. Are the debates about life or the afterlife?"

"It turns out, both."

"Oh."

"Let's take me, for example," he said. "I was born in 1881 and lived until 1949. Was that too soon, or just right?"

"But you lived in a different time, Sir," Ty answered. "Sixty-eight was considered a long life in those days."

"Miss, believe me, I felt it was a long life. I was ready to go. But now you just passed away and you were ninety! It would have been unfathomable to my world, but this was your reality. I ask you then: At ninety, were you ready?"

Ty sighed deeply and closed her eyes. "I was so bored for so long."

"But if you had died any sooner, say at sixty-eight, your children would have been very alarmed. The coroner would have had to look for an illness that caused the death. When I died, though, everyone agreed it was simply old age. And we were all at peace with that."

"That's all history is," Madame Kim said. "A foreign civilization to all who come after it." She had appeared with a little blue-and-white porcelain tray. From it, she took a matching miniature pot, poured a clear liquid into a miniature cup, and offered it with both hands to the ancient scholar. Then she asked the others. "Would you like some rice wine, Madame Ty? No? Madame Mary? No?" She put the tray on the table, poured herself a cup then settled into the other side chair.

Kim's husband, Tien, said from the bar, "Excuse my second wife. She's obsessed with the context of each generation." He glanced at the scholar and was relieved his father was not offended.

"But Madame Kim is right," Tai said, lighting cigarettes for those around the bar and a cigarillo for himself. "It *is* context." He takes a deep drag from the tobacco. "I mean, I was only fifty-three when I died. Son-in-law Nghia was fifty-eight. Was our time too soon?"

Anne blew a smoke ring. "I was seventy-six."

Kim sipped her rice wine. "I was eighty-three."

Mary looked at Ty. "I was eighty-one. Out of the grandmothers, you lived the longest."

"But you said that wasn't living. You think that the last decade of mine was ... dead!"

"Oh no, I was ... I was talking about Hal," Mary stammered, shaking her head and looking around to the others for help. "Ninety seems to be the norm these days. And he's almost there. That was all I was saying."

The old scholar leaned back in his chair. "Ninety does seem to be the norm this day and age. In the sixty years since my death, medical breakthroughs and modern diets have improved quality of life beyond what people in my days could have imagined." He chuckled. "I've even heard on TV that sixty-five is the new fifty. If only I had lived long enough."

"Sir," Ty said, "you said you were ready to go."

"And so I was. Which brings me to this level of the netherworld." He put his blue-and-white porcelain cup back on the tray and poured himself more rice wine. "I've been thinking it's probably time for me to exit this stage. Among the souls on this altar, after all, I've been a ghost the longest. Granted, it's a wide, wide world, and it has taken my spirit all this time to discover all its nooks and crannies. Not only in geography, mind you." Nguyen Xuan Trach smiled at Vu Thi Ty. "One of the wonders you'll discover, Miss, is reading via what the living are reading. It's like having this vast library of my own, in languages I never learned!"

Anne said, "Sir, don't forget watching TV. Even you have been fascinated by some of these modern reality shows!" She grinned at Ty. "My daughter's hooked on them, and we like to watch TV with Carol Anne."

"And don't forget these computers," said Carroll, as he read one of the screens set up on the dining table. He smiled at Ty. "We like it when the living forget to turn off the computers. During the day, we watch how they use these machines, then we try to do the same thing when they're asleep."

Before Ty could sort out all the images she was receiving, the old scholar said, "As you can see, we all have been enjoying these modern times through the living. I learn a lot this way about the brave new world. But what I enjoy even more is when I get to learn about science, especially space and time."

Try as she might, Ty couldn't help groaning in her mind.

The old scholar laughed. "That's all right, Miss Ty. Allow me to —"

He stopped. Madame Ty looked at Nghia's paternal grandfather and followed his gaze toward the bar. Her husband and the others have parted, and in their midst, a figure in a thick, cream robe is pouring cognac into a square glass.

"How fortuitous," the scholar continued. "Allow me, then, to use her as an example. Now, she doesn't believe in God or Buddha. Actually, at one point, she used to believe in both! But no more."

"Who is she?" Ty asked. "What does she believe in?"

The Force, the old souls in the room think in unison, their eyes on the one not even acknowledging their presence.

"What do you mean The Force? As in 'Star Wars'?"

"Good for you, Miss! I knew you'd remember from watching TV with our grandchildren."

"It's an American movie, not a religion," she said patronizingly to Mr. Tai.

But it was the old scholar who laughed. "Yes, a movie, but one based on science and philosophy, if I understand correctly from reading interviews with the director — through the living, of course." His eyes twinkled. "But think about it. All life forms contain matter created in the Big Bang. When the body dies, our particles float up, or out, or inward, what have you. Those particles could make up a spirit, say, who once in a while could be seen by the living! That's what we could be made of right now. Or those particles could join other particles that make up other souls. You have enough spirits and energy particles floating out there in the atmosphere, amidst the stars, or deep in the earth's crust, or percolating inside the bodies of mortals or whatever, and there's The Force, strong enough to once in a while affect the living and their environment. Miss Ty, why not?"

"That's what she believes in?"

Her husband, who couldn't take his eyes off this young woman, shrugged. "It's not *not* true."

The figure in the thick robe, so disrespectfully oblivious to her elders, approached the altar.

Madame Ty looked at the scholar. "Sir, I can't believe ..."

"Well, her father-in-law, Mary's son, believes in reincarnation."

"No, Sir, I mean how disrespectful ... What did you just say? Whose son is Buddhist?" She looked at Mary.

But it's son-in-law Nghia who answered. "Mother, Big Bob has visions that he and I, in a past life many, many moons ago, were Catholic monks together in some Italian monastery. Once in a while, I still see him dreaming that dream in which he sees himself covered in a brown burlap robe with his feet in homemade sandals. And then I see myself in his dream. We're picking olives together and are very close friends. Who knows, we might have owed each other for some reason or another from that former life, and maybe it's why our children are married in this one."

Ty closed her eyes and tried harder to concentrate. "Mary, were you not a Christian?"

"I still am."

Ty looked at her. Have you seen your Maker then?

Mary shook her head.

"Come to think of it, Sir," Ty addressed the scholar, "you were Buddhist." She looked around at the other souls. "Most of you were. What happened at your hundredth-day ceremony? What were the judgments on your souls? Why aren't any of you reincarnated yet?"

The old gentleman stared at her. Has it been a hundred days?

"Yes, of course." It has most definitely been a hundred days times a hundredth, thousandth, and umpteen millionth times over for everyone on the altar.

The old gentleman sighed. On whose calendar, Miss? That's what I've been wondering. On whose calendar?

Ty closed her eyes again.

"Miss, I'm sorry I'm hurting your head. But it's a question that has been preoccupying me. I lived sixty-eight years as a mortal. Well, based on the mortal calendar, it has been more than sixty years I've been hanging around this stage of the afterlife. I'm ready to go. I'm eager to find out what's next. What if there are multiple stages of this netherworld? What if this is our waiting room, before meeting the higher-ups? No matter the God you believe in. I now have a mortal decade to prepare for the next level, don't you see? Whereas for you, Miss, the number is ninety. Will you still want to be here by then? Or will you be like me, ready for the next world at sixty?"

Mary said softly, "And now we're back comparing Hal with you, Sir."

"You're right. What's too soon, and what's just right? How long is long enough, whether in life, or afterlife? Don't get me wrong, Miss Ty, this altar is ... family; you'll be happy here, good companionship, and I've learned a lot from visiting other altars at the homes of other descendants. Even so, to use the American lingo, when the party's over, it's time to go."

Carroll laughed. "Good one, Sir! But I'd miss you." He raised his glass.

The oldest spirit in the room smiled and continued: "What if, to get to the next level, we have to find a door to enter? A door we souls can't see. You have to feel The Force to find it. Or a spirit from there could guide you to it, much like your husband helping you find the white door to this space."

"What if you don't?"

The scholar laughed. "I've been having fun trying. That alone has been worth it."

Ty looked around at the non-Asians. "Aren't any of you worried? Why are you so comfortable if there's no Heaven or Hell? What if you run out of time trying to find the next level?"

Mary shook her head. "Oh no, Ty, time is not of the essence. Faith is. God is bigger than any calendar man created. Man's time is not God's time."

"But Mary, what if there is no God? How long are you willing to wait here before you find out?"

The white-haired woman smiled — no, she *glowed* — all uncertainty gone from her face and voice. "Ty, I'm not just sitting around waiting. There are so many places I never felt brave enough to explore when I was mortal, so much to discover about this afterlife, and all of humanity to visit and learn from. I'm occupied and perfectly content. I'm in no hurry, and God will come for me when He's ready."

***

The one in white put her drink on the altar. She opened a drawer and pulled out three incense sticks. She lit them, closed her eyes, and held them up to her forehead, whispering something Ty couldn't quite catch even with her new powers. She planted the smoking sticks into a porcelain bowl full of rice grains and already burned-out incense, then put her hands together and bowed three times.

It's up to the self to know the self
And I know my own self

Mr. Tai!

Ha! It was granddaughter Thuan who led you here after all. Do you recognize her, Miss? He chuckled. You faked it pretty well the last time she visited you in Arizona.

Thuan left the room, her mind still filled with that folk song, and Madame Ty followed the firstborn of her firstborn.

One embraces all forms of life
Lying inside a woeful sound
Look, there are still so many people
Guiding one another 'round here

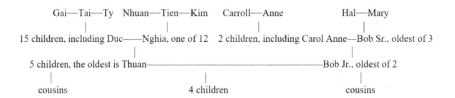

***

Thuan entered a room where, on a giant TV screen, giant men in long shorts are mutedly fighting over a bouncing ball. In front of a fireplace in which red embers are still smoldering, a man had fallen asleep on the brown sofa. Gently, she lifted the remote control from his chest to turn off the television.

Ty felt the other grandmothers joining her. Anne and Mary asked, "Do you recognize our grandson?"

I do now. Bob was known in our clan as the American son-in-law who can speak Vietnamese. Ty smiled.

And heard Kim guffawing next to her. You should have heard him when he first visited me in Thu Duc, tones and accents in all the wrong places. But I have to admit that by the time he left after two years, he sounded almost a local.

Ty shushed Kim. Aren't you afraid of waking him?

Kim touched her arm. Have you forgotten we're just old ghosts?

Ty looked at her, dumbstruck. Kim's coiled raven hair was now snow white, her smooth face wrinkled and shrunken. Ty turned to the American women and saw that Hollywood Anne had aged as well, matching Mary's grandmotherly visage.

Your turn, Anne said.

Involuntarily, Ty felt her body grow rounder, her muscles and joints ached, her skin sagged all over, and her teeth — they were all gone.

It was so dark all of a sudden. The other grandmothers floated toward the light in an adjacent space. From which Ty heard a flickering flute, then a mournful mandolin:

Embracing the heart of night
Watching the arrival of a new moon
Nostalgia for the drifter

Oh, ephemeral time
As each spring ages
One day you reach shore
A human life passes like a breeze

I know that ballad, Ty thought, crossing the sliding glass door into a room wrapped in windows. It was another song written by Trinh Cong Son and sung by that smoky Khanh-Ly.

Thuan was curled up on a high couch, its dark wood carved, and its beige cushion covered with pillows. The ballad came from a stereo in the corner, above which shone a huge, round, paper lantern. Ty sat next to her granddaughter, who was sipping cognac as she scribbled in a book bound in silk the color of new leaves.

There are many times
From the midnight garden stepping home
Whose feet are ever so gentle
As if kissing yesteryears

Ty frowned. Why is she listening to this?

Anne rolled her eyes. Be grateful. You wouldn't want to hear the horrible noise my grandson listens to, electric guitars and screaming.

Actually, said Kim, you wouldn't believe Thuan's taste in Vietnamese music. Nothing recorded after '75. Too much ... synthesizer, that was her reasoning, not enough real instruments.

I mean, why is our granddaughter listening to such a sad song? Is she not happy?

Anne sighed. Much happier than I was.

Kim, browsing through a shelf of colorful plastic containers holding toy trains, blocks, plastic groceries, and cloth books, mumbled, "I've heard her tell Bob that his fathering style has made her a better mother. Could any of us say that about our husbands?"

"Actually, yes." Mary sat next to her new friend on the high sofa. "Ty, Hal loved raising kids. Now he lives for the great-grandkids. I really do think that's where my two Bobs got it from; they love fatherhood. You shouldn't worry. Thuan took me to a movie once that made me question her. But Thuan's blessed and she knows it. There's no suffering, trust me. Not like how each of us had to deal with ... things. This music, Thuan just wanted to listen to something that would make her feel close to you, that's all. Her thoughts are full of you right now. Don't forget, she's in mourning. Just look at her journal."

Ty, feeling guilty but curious all the same, leaned into the green book.

12:41 a.m. Wednesday 1/28/09

It's been snowing. A couple of inches out there on the deck, in the yard. Everyone is asleep.

Our flight landed at 3 p.m. at Washington Dulles, and the kids were so excited. The 2-year-old kept staring out the plane window saying, "Snow! Snow!"

I'm so drained, physically and emotionally, from the trip to AZ. As soon as I saw the open casket Friday evening, I knew she was gone. That wasn't her in there, the skin no longer felt like her skin, her cheeks were wax, her hands were cold. What was there, what was alive, was the joy and curiosity of seeing family and friends I hadn't seen for too long. And it was so much fun to watch my kids interact with everyone. They've been hearing about this huge family for years, but this was the first time they've seen most of us in one place. It was like a big party. I didn't cry at all at the funeral on Saturday.

When was the last time I was in AZ for Tet? I can't even remember. This year, Tet fell on Monday, 1/26. No. 1 priority would have been to go wish Ba Ngoai a Happy New Year. But she's no longer there. The realization didn't hit me until Sunday, right in the middle of the first post-funeral service at the Buddhist temple. The monk is chanting; my mind's bored so it starts to wander, thinking that it's New Year's Eve and what I should do for the rest of the day, going over all the planned family activities and wondering how to squeeze in a visit to Ba Ngoai. Then I started sobbing and couldn't stop, like an idiot, and one of my aunts had to pass me a whole box of tissue.

What a weekend. Mourning and celebrating at the same time.

1954 − 1918 = 36

Only 36! That's how old Ba Ngoai was when she and Ong Ngoai fled the north and lost everything but their children!

What was Ba Ngoai doing at my age?

1918 + 42 = 1960

She was still trying to rebuild their lives in the south — and trying to feed and clothe all those children. At 42, she had her last child, a son. And it's two years away from her husband's death.

Ty lifted her eyes from the green book to her granddaughter. "How? How did I have all those children? And your Ong Ngoai, he just gave up and drank himself to death so he wouldn't have to deal with any of it!"

Hush. Mary was alarmed. Why are you yelling? It wasn't her fault.

No? Didn't we live so they could live? What an unending chain. Now she's suffering so her children could live.

But I already told you. She has it much better than we had it.

Oh no, I know this granddaughter, longer than you have. She's just like my husband. I understand her. I hear her! "He's trouble when everything is fine. The need to destroy things creeps up on him every time." Ty stopped, confused by the foreign words that just came out of her mouth.

Anne coughed. Madame, are you accusing your husband and me of something?

Kim, on the other hand, was laughing. "Ri Lo ... Ri Lo Ki Ley? You're using some American band's lyrics from Thuan's memory against your Vietnamese husband? Heaven, you really are getting into her head."

Ty frowned. Stop laughing at me. Stop picking on me just because I don't know what I'm doing. Why am I here?

Because you've died, the other grandmothers sighed. Now you must go through what we did.

Ty clicked her tongue impatiently. What does that mean? What happens next? You don't even know what's going on with Heaven or Hell. Nobody here has the answer. Not even the scholar.

Granddaughter Thuan suddenly looked up, back into the TV room. Bob had awakened in the dark, yawning. She asked him, "What time is it?"

"Time to end the night." He rose.

The soul in the cream robe gathered her things, then turned off the stereo and the lights before joining her husband.

Ty followed the couple, the three other spirits close behind.

As they crossed the sliding glass door in the dark, Anne whispered, "Repentance."

On the way out of the TV room, Kim sighed, "Judgment."

In the entryway, in front of the white door and the silent knight, Mary promised, "Deliverance."

Thuan stopped at the altar. The dead were gone from the now-darkened living room, but Madame Ty could feel their silent eyes staring out of the picture frames. Thuan lit another three incense sticks. After planting them, she reached into the top shelf and tenderly straightened one of the frames.

It's me, Ty realized. She looked from the granddaughter in white back to her own picture on the altar. How did you get my French colonial ID card? How did you get that little photo to grow ten times its size?

Bob touched Thuan's shoulder, guiding his wife toward the dark staircase. Madame Ty glided up after them. From below, her fellow grandmothers gave her one last word: Acceptance.

But the white-haired woman wasn't really listening. Because she saw her own husband waiting at the top of the stairs — not the arrogant young man in the silk suit, but a shy old man in plain cotton.

* * *

"Would you like to see our firstborn?" he asked her.

She followed her husband into a room where son-in-law Nghia was already waiting. On a four-poster bed, a salt-and-pepper-haired woman lay sleeping with a small boy. Behind them, on a light blue mural, a fawn rested on a patch of grass as a bunny tried to talk it into coming out to play.

"See, Miss," Mr. Tai said, "Duc's a grandmother herself now."

"It's a miracle she's managed to become a grandmother after the way you insisted on raising her as a boy, trying to make up for your already having daughters even before you married me ... from her cropped hair to her boyish shorts, to how you kept telling her that boys don't cry."

"Are you scolding me about that again? I gave up after Duc entered school, didn't I?"

"By then it was too late, Mr. Tai, don't you see? She's always been too boyish. Even in her maiden teens, she thought nothing about tying up the two panels of her white, high school ao dai so she could ride her bike home from school more comfortably."

Nghia chuckled. "Mother, it might be that my wife is practical and quick on her feet. And it's true she's blunt in her words and quick to frown on people who can't control their emotions. I remember one of those rare times our children really saw her cry, it alarmed them because it was so unlike her."

"Last time I remember her crying was at your funeral."

"Mother, it was our first winter in America. People from the church that sponsored our family rang the doorbell one night and brought in Christmas. All of Christmas — a tree they taught our kids to decorate right then, presents to put under it, cookies. It was the first time I tried eggnog. In the middle of all this, the pastor's wife suddenly asked where Duc had gone. When the kids found her, she was in our bedroom crying. She just couldn't believe that people who looked absolutely nothing like us and who weren't connected to us by blood at all could be so kind. It was a very movie sort of scene, Mother. The spirit of Christmas just like those American films that managed to make it to Sai Gon all those years ago: the pastor's wife coming into the bedroom to comfort my wife and bringing Duc back out to the living room, then everybody coming up to hug her. It was hilarious. The idea that my wife, rarely affectionate even with our own children, was being wrapped in the arms of all these foreign men and women! The memory still tickles me."

Mr. Tai sat on the bed and — with a gentleness not human — stroked the boy's head, so that in the toddler's sleep if he felt the touch at all it might have been a draft coming through a crack in the window. "Elder brother Nghia, tell your mother-in-law how Duc is with her own grandchildren."

"Mother, it's true. Duc is a different woman. She hugs our grandchildren more than I've ever seen her touching anyone. She praises them more than she ever praised our own children."

"Miss, in the end, the grandchildren have raised her better than we did."

"Are you blaming me?" Ty stared at her husband. You think you were a better father than I was a mother? Forget what they said at my funeral, you should have heard what they said at yours.

Nghia faded from the room.

Trust me, I was there. I heard. Sighing, Mr. Tai slowly looked up at his wife. Miss, but you'll realize, sooner or later our children's judgment will matter no more. I now see myself through the eyes of our grandchildren and great-grandchildren and so on. I mean, I was among the fourteenth generation of an ancestor who was the education minister at the royal court, Duc was the fifteenth and that little boy there is of the seventeenth generation. A royal court that no longer exists, a mandarin whose dust sleeps with the ages. It's very humbling that our world is gone and I'm no longer the central character, the man of the house, the head of the clan.

Humbling? Astonished that her husband would even use such a word about himself, she spoke, "You're drunk. You always did get philosophical when you got drunk."

"Yes. I was a drunk. That's a fact."

His eyes wandered around their daughter's room. Silently, he directed Madame Ty to gaze at one of the many photos covering the walls. In a black-and-white picture, a girl with short hair and bangs straight across her forehead stared resentfully out at the world: Duc at four years old. Mr. Tai looked from the photo back to the grandmother Duc had become.

Miss, haunting our children all these years — watching them escape communism, adapt to a foreign continent, raise kids in culture shock, build entire new lives — I've learned a lot. You and I, we had our own hardships together, it's true. We also fled from communism, but at least we technically stayed in the same land, not really having to learn a new language. In many ways, our descendants have had to deal with much more. Do you understand?

Madame Ty willed herself to be still, watching in fascination as her husband uncharacteristically struggled to express himself.

Mr. Tai folded his arms and continued out loud. "Agreed, our children chose their lives, more or less. So did we, through all our individual decisions. All these choices in our marriage, we made them. Then life happened, then you had to make a decision about how to adapt or change your life.

"Look at Duc there. She chose a husband; we didn't arrange it. She waited for him to come back from graduate school and officer training, not us. Yes, she has had her ups and downs in life, in which *she* is the central character. I can't tell you how much my spirit moaned that whole night Nghia fell into a coma and then died of a brain aneurysm, leaving our daughter a widow. I suffered for her pain! In the eyes of her grandchildren, though, Duc is just a supporting character. They're blissfully unaware of who she is and what she has been through.

"Just imagine, then, how unimportant we are. For the great-grandchildren, I'm just a black-and-white picture on the altar. Now, so are you."

Madame Ty shook her head. The anger she had been burying all these years was filling her chest and threatening to detonate. But she forced herself to look at her husband. And seeing him — really seeing Mr. Tai's soul there in front of her — her rage suddenly disintegrated. She sighed, listening to the breathing of her daughter and great-grandson. What was the point? What had she been expecting from him all these years?

She turned away. I understand. I chose you, which meant I chose my fate and whatever you brought with it. Now life is done. I simply lived out my destiny. I see. It was a good lesson.

That wasn't what I meant at all! Mr. Tai lowered his eyes. "What I'm trying to say is — what really happened was —"

Behind his spoken words, the direction of his mind arrested her attention. Ever so slowly, so as not to chase away his thoughts, Madame Ty lowered herself onto the bed and looked at Mr. Tai.

Miss, you know what I mean. You can read my mind now.

Sir, you've been reading my mind for years.

Nguyen Huu Tai looked down at the descendants lying between him and Vu Thi Ty, then he looked his wife in the eye. I'm sorry.

Madame Ty grimaced, trying not to sob. Thank you, Sir. Thank you.

Mr. Tai reached for her hands. I beg you, don't cry. Forgive me.

She shook her head. There's nothing to forgive. We did the best we could.

Startled by her uncharacteristic surrender, he stood and pulled her to him. Not I. But I'm stronger now, you'll see. You were strong in life, and now I can be strong for you in death. I've had all these years to figure out how things should work.

Madame Ty leaned into Mr. Tai's shoulders, a gesture so rare when they were alive that now it was like seeing an exotic bud open. The weight of her made him laugh out loud. Not caring about waking the living at all.

Vu Thi Ty died January 17, 2009, in Arizona. Survivors included her youngest sister, a resident of Northern Virginia; fifteen children and ten of their spouses; forty-six grandchildren and their spouses; nineteen great-grandchildren; two great-great-grandchildren; and nieces and nephews. In November 2010, her four sons brought her ashes back to northern Viet Nam to scatter into Ha Long Bay.

Eleven

January 17, 2009, was a Saturday night. Daddy and I and his parents had taken out-of-town friends to dinner. When we came home, all the lights were on and incense had been lit on the altar, though you children and my mother were supposed to be asleep already. Before I could question what was going on, Ba rushed down the stairs saying, "Thuan, get me a flight to Arizona. Ba Ngoai has died!"

We immediately went to the computers on the dining table. Daddy said he'd order the ticket online, so I called my sister. And my sister ... my sister answered that one of our brothers had already posted the news on Facebook.

I had to repeat it to myself and instantly recoiled. I wasn't on Facebook then. Except for e-mail, I wasn't a social media citizen then. I was pissed. You don't find out on Facebook that your grandmother died. Maybe it's how you find out when other people's grandmothers die, but not your own.

It's now 1:40 a.m. January 17, 2015, the very first hour and minutes of another Saturday. The whole house is asleep, and I'm standing here by the light of the incense on the altar, looking into the portraits of my Ba Ngoai, my Ong Ngoai.

His eyes warn: You make your habits, then your habits make you.

Her eyes, on the other hand, are encouraging: You make a life with someone, then at some point, you must earn it.

I scan all the other portraits on the family altar, the Vietnamese ones

186

in black and white, the Americans in full color. Did they earn it? How did they pursue their happiness? Who knew how often each of them had to cross Contrary Creek, take Last Chance Road, climb Think It Over Hill? But they did it. Why, or for whom? Did it matter anymore?

***

RE: Ba Ngoai
Sunday, April 26, 2009 3:43 PM
From: <tina@Thumbelina.net>
To: <inspiredfollies@hotmail.com>
living with grandma was way more fun when we were younger. she would cook for us and we would play games and cards. i would say around high school it got worse. her memory faded and she would scream and scream all around the house, especially in the bathroom mirror to herself. tony and i could never have friends over. i could never have my boyfriends over because it was chaos. she would leave all the lights on, move things around, flush the toilet continuously for no reason. it raised my dad's electricity and utility bills astronomically. she would be really mean to us, too. i know it wasn't her fault, it was just because she was getting older and didn't really know what was going on. we had to lock everything up, we had to put in locked doorknobs and we had to carry our own key to our rooms because she would go to my room or tony's and just take things and hoard them, like my jewelry or cash. but yea it got really bad for a while and my mom had to mostly do it on her own until ba lived with bac toan.

anyway, hope life is good. i loved the easter pics on facebook!

RE: Ba Ngoai
Monday, April 27, 2009 12:40 AM
From: <tony@youdontknowme.org>
To: <inspiredfollies@hotmail.com>
Well, living with grandma has been something. From the moment I could really remember anything, it was her. She babysat me when my parents were out working, and Tina was in school. She took care of me, taught me lessons,

and how to value and cherish things. Told me everything about our incredibly huge family. I thought we were in like a serious family mafia or something. She would watch Power Rangers *in the morning with me and I would watch* Wheel of Fortune *with her at night. She bought me my PlayStation when my parents didn't, which I will NEVER sell ... ever.*

But then when I was around maybe 12-13, Grandma started getting a bit sick. Not physically but mentally. She was actually in amazing health for a 90-year-old lady, even to the day she died. She started talking to herself more often and I got kinda scared. In the middle of almost every night, you can hear her screaming at herself in the mirror. Just babbling to herself. She didn't know that the lady in the mirror was her anymore.

Then about two years ago, she went to go live with Aunty Toan. After that, when I would go to visit her she didn't even recognize/remember me.

* * *

When I e-mailed my cousins soon after Ba Ngoai's funeral to ask what it was like living with our maternal grandmother, I didn't know what to expect. Except honesty. And they didn't disappoint. What was more tragic? Two little kids whose doting grandmother could no longer recognize them, or a woman whose grandchildren will remember her more for how she died than for how she lived?

Wow, I thought, what a fitting ending to the story of Vu Thi Ty.

Lately, though ... in my darkest out-of-body moments, haunting my own house at night as I readjusted bookshelves, lit incense to the ancestors, looked into my children's faces as they slept, poked at the burning wood in the fireplace until it bled hot red guts and released golden stars ... I thought about those e-mails and questioned, why try? Why accomplish anything? Why live for anyone but myself if all they remembered was my ignoble end?

Then I'd hear such laughter, loud and loose. I'd see all those black-and-white, color, Vietnamese, and American faces on the altar loving me and mocking me at the same time: Why, why, why? Whine, whine, whine.

Last autumn was a nightmare, and I'm not tossing that word out there lightly. Boom, out of nowhere, like a grenade. My mother — Duc — and I spent a harrowing week at Georgetown hospital after she had an eight-hour colon surgery that involved a blood transfusion. Each night, I'd sleep on a recliner next to her gurney wishing that she and I could wake up in our own beds. But each day dawned with rounds of nurses and doctors, and the day would be measured in IV drips, blood pressures, hemoglobin levels, breathing exercises, and physical therapy. Then the sun would sink, and the cycle started all over the next day, and the next.

Ba despaired of ever getting out of there. But escape she did, free of cancer and free of chemotherapy, just barely.

Now that she has recovered — taking care of herself again, walking again, playing cards with her friends again, driving herself to a Buddhist temple again — do you know what that means? I have my mother again. Five words, five words I'll never say lightly again, ever. Just five words separate her from life and death. Living, it's how I want to remember my mother, and not those dark ignoble days in the hospital.

Aspiration — how can a word full of hope be linked to such foreboding? But Webster's New World dictionary, our shared public history, defines aspiration as:

1) strong desire or ambition, as for advancement, honor, etc.;

2) the thing so desired;

3) a breathing in, as of dust into the lungs;

4) removal of fluid or gas by suction, as from a body cavity.

As it happens, your Great-Grandpa Hal's throat muscle is no longer working, so food and liquid are getting into his lungs. His caregivers have to be extra careful when they feed him now, so he won't choke to death. How's that for living?

As a new parent, you stare into the fire and hope that your children will live wonderful lives.

As an old child, I now stare into the flames and hope that my aging loved ones will die a peaceful death.

When I think about my mother and my grandfather-in-law, do I really want to live into my 90s?

You're right. I hear you. A lot of things can happen in four decades. Till then ...

Where are you reading this? Who have you become? In what cul-de-sac of history are you living as you learn about your past, something old that's suddenly new? I can't picture you at all.

Try to picture me, more than my beginning, more than my ending.

Acknowledgements

Me, my wonder woman mother who gave me life and then taught me how to live.

My super parents-in-law, who not only agreed to live with us all these years as a multigenerational and multicultural family, but also gamely shared their family stories.

My brothers and sister, and aunts, uncles, and cousins worldwide, for their continued generosity, guidance, critiques, laughter, and memories.

Trinh Vinh Trinh and Nguyen Trung Truc of the Trinh Cong Son family and foundation, for the copyright permission to the artist's lyrics from the songs "Ngau Nhien" and "Phoi Pha."

The haunting Rilo Kiley, for the band's OK and "Good Luck!"

Justin Bonfiglio, copyright specialist at the University of Michigan Library, for his guidance.

And Bob, my patient and adventurous road trip partner through life, for never stopping to court each other.

About the Author

Thuan Le Elston was born in South Vietnam, and her family left a week before Saigon fell in 1975. A former *Los Angeles Times* reporter, she has been a member of the *USA Today* Editorial Board since 2005. One of her few non-journalism jobs was a speaking role in Oliver Stone's movie *Heaven and Earth*.

CPSIA information can be obtained
at www.ICGtesting.com
Printed in the USA
BVHW040756130921
616660BV00014B/191